Wrecked

by

Nick Stephens

Sometimes, in the midst of the storm, the thunder is crashing all around you like the drums of death and the lightning striking relentlessly like the fires of hell, but the rain... the rain feels like the resurrection of life. Piecing you back together.

Prologue

I'm not a monster. I'm not anything really. I'm not anything until the time calls for it. Then, I am whatever is needed of me. I'll do whatever needs to be done to protect what's mine, but please understand, it is always what NEEDS to be done. I don't enjoy doing these things. Well, that's a lie. I enjoy some of it. I suppose you get a taste for things after a while. Bloodshed and vengeance are like wine in that way. It burns going down the first few sips, but the more you drink, the smoother it gets until it becomes something your palate looks forward to tasting.

So, maybe I am a monster. The question then is, did I create myself, or am I the manifestation of the rage within the people surrounding me? And then, if it's the latter, aren't those people the true monsters? Afterall, it was they who breathed life into me. I say that not to pass blame though. Existence is funny that way. Ask yourself, *if given the choice to create a life reflecting the worst in me, would I do it?* Doubtful.

Yet here I am just the same. The biproduct of inhumanity. I'm not saying this to garner pity. I don't have any feelings about it one way or the other. I'm merely sharing my contemplations, not that you asked. Early on, I was bitter. Asking existential questions about why I was created in such a horrendous condition. Perhaps that's why I began to project myself to people as a gentle creature. You see, when you spend as much time as I have alone in the darkness, you eventually come to terms with things and realize that there is no explanation for our existence. So, there's no use worrying about why we are the way we are. Getting upset by your nature is like being angry at a bee for stinging you.

So, why am I here? Same reason as you I suppose.

The sun's rays were like jellyfish by the thousands, stinging Sam's already blistered skin. His lips dry and deeply cratered like the Mojave Desert valleys, and he could hardly feel the sand fleas feasting on his legs anymore. He closed his eyes for, what he hoped was, one final sleep.

Cool air began to wash over him like a cocoon, but he was ripped back to reality by the sound of another man shouting. Slowly, Sam opened his eyes. He felt like a prisoner, who had been condemned to solitary confinement, finally being let back into general population. He squinted against the light and saw the source of the voice previously in his head. Was it God? The Devil? Would Sam know the difference? So long as he wasn't alone on this island any longer, he didn't care.

"Wham!" A small boat crashed ashore like it accidentally discovered America. The jolt made the occupant fall headfirst into the tide. The man stumbled a few feet before dropping limply to the tide's edge. Running on pure instinct and adrenaline, Sam shot from death to the other man's side and pulled him to land. The man was hyperventilating like a scolded child as he lay otherwise motionless in the sand. A few heaving breaths later, he blacked out. It only took Sam a split second to realize that this man, this boat, offered no rescue. Then he blacked out too.

Sam awoke several hours later under some giant palm leaves to the sound of Desmond's voice grumbling. In his grogginess he had a dreamlike sensation that he was a little kid listening to the sound of his father shouting in the distance. No, not his father, but familiar, nonetheless. As Sam gained focus, he saw Desmond. He leaned up against a palm trunk with a groan and observed. Desmond was maybe 10-15 years older than Sam, and his clothes were completely tattered. Dangling from his cargo shorts on a rope was a rabbit's foot. Aimless or on a mission, Desmond was shifting back and forth swiftly moving wood and other indiscernible things around on the beach. Suddenly, as if on a pivot, Desmond turned and b-lined it over to Sam.

"Oh! Wakey wakey!" Desmond coaxed as he leaned in. "Thanks for the rescue, mate!"

Sam recognized the irony in Desmond's word choice.

"Sure." he grumbled.

"Name's Desmond but call me Des." he offered. "How long you been on this rock?"

Desmond handed Sam some berries and some edible flowers.

(Made himself right at home, huh?)

Sam adjusted his back against the tree, grabbed the offering with one hand, and put his other hand over his eyes to block the sun.

"Thanks. I crash landed here about 3 months ago, I think. I lost track of few days here and there. You're the first sign of human life I've come across since I got here. Aside from the birds and monsters in the woods."

Sam didn't mention how he ended up on the island. That's because Sam couldn't remember.

"I don't doubt that, mate. You're off the grid." Desmond's right eye twitched in flutters like a rabbit's nose. He spoke hurried, erratic. Sam couldn't place an accent, but Desmond used mixed up slang and gestures like he was character morphing.

Sam wondered how he could know where they were but left it alone. The sun was already at mid-morning and despite the berries, his stomach was howling like a junkyard dog at midnight. He reached for a coconut and went for the knife on his hip.

"I got it, fella!' Desmond urged and in one motion snatched the coconut from Sam with one hand and with the other, drew the but-end of a serrated combat knife into the coconut shell like a gavel of final judgment before taking a swig of the juice within.

Sam looked perplexed and, kind-of pissed off, at his knife in Desmond's hand. Desmond noticed. He twisted the knife in his hand like a baton and offered it back to Sam.

"There ya go. She's still intact."

Sam forgave the transgression and moved on.

"Well, I guess that means you aren't the search party then?" Sam jested.

"No such luck. We were on a vessel northwest of here." He pointed deliberately in the direction from which he came, and then continued.

"Storm damn near threw us into the abyss, but it'll take a lot more than a lil' sky piss to knock the vinegar out of this old salt…

(Talk like a normal person…)

"We managed to swim to that dingy and we've been floating around on her ever since." He pointed toward the boat that brought him there.

"So I'm guessing the island isn't inhabited then?" Desmond continued.

"Population, one." Sam offered.

"Been in there yet, then?" Desmond nodded toward the jungle.

Sam still felt weak. The sun danced across his eyes obnoxiously. He squinted more. His sand coated eyelashes were rusty bars caging his pupils.

"I've only been a few hundred yards into the jungle. I didn't want to stray too far from my signal fire and risk it going out in case a ship or a plane or a UFO passed by. Plus, it gets really hairy the farther in you go. Thick with these thorny vine things. I got wrapped up in them a few days after I got here and they damn near ripped my skin to shreds." Sam ran his hands along his ribs where soft scabs from his ordeal remained. "One of my shoes is still in there somewhere…"

Sam trailed for a few seconds and his eyes met Desmond's mid-section where a chunk of his shirt was torn. He noticed a long scarring scab almost mirroring his beneath the cloth.

"And then there were the strange markings and stuff," he continued. "… and some howling screams. It was enough to keep me from going too deep again."

"Strange markings and howling screams, eh?" Desmond questioned.

Desmond went from standing over Sam to sitting chummy by his side, hanging on Sam's words as if he were whispering the secrets of the universe.

"Yea. I can't really describe them except for saying it's scary enough to keep me out of there if I can help it. Unlike any animal I've ever heard. And the trees shake something terrible too. Reminds me of some J.J. Abrams movie or something."

"A monster then, eh?

"Maybe." Sam trailed.

"I mean, I have my knife" he motioned to the knife Desmond had made himself familiar with, "And this makeshift backup." Sam reached into his cargo shorts pocket and pulled out a crusty old toothbrush with a jagged edge. "But it's not much protection from whatever's lurking out there. Luckily, I found some edible plants, berries, and coconuts closer to the beach. Since then, I decided to build my shelter at the tree line here and I've pretty much stuck to the outer edges of the jungle, rationing what I find. And there is a small water source around that bend right there. Some sort of water pocket that fills up from a small waterfall. It's clean from the fall but I'd steer clear of drinking it from the base where it's settled. That's kept me alive-ish."

Desmond was almost smiling. One of those smiles that people get when they are anticipating hearing an announcement that they've just won something lifechanging, but they are trying to hold it back as to not jinx it.

"Alive alright!" Desmond cheered with an elbow to Sam's scabbed up ribs.

"Seems like you've been making out alright. Right plump for the skewer, you are." Desmond certainly had a way with words.

"We made out alright out in the drink as well. I mean there were no hairy Monsters or thorny jungle traps to compete with out there. Just a sea creature or two and that ball of spitfire…" Des pointed to the sun. "And the occasional bout of the freak-out staring into the nothing." He chuckled. "It was enough to get your panties in a bunch. Good thing I'm a good conversationalist or we woulda ended up a little *One Flew Over the Coo-Coo's Nest* out there, right?" Again, he laughed. Caught up in Desmond's oddities, Sam laughed a bit too.

"So…what happened out there?" Sam questioned.

"Well, we were on a fishing trip. I was supposed to catch a prize, ya know. Gut it, clean it, mount it on the wall for my wife to see."

Sam cleared his throat.

"I had everything ready and baited just right waiting for a bite when there was a screeching sound from the engine and then, *KABLOOWEY!*" Desmond threw his hands together in a clap in front of his face and continued to throw his hands up in the air in the shape of a mushroom cloud.

"The charter was ablaze faster than the underbrush in a California forest. It was a free-for-all after that. We got that trolling boat into the water and hightailed it outta there…floated about for some time. I did catch that prize though."

"The fish?" Sam asked confusedly.

"Right!", Desmond continued. "Well, we better get to it and not muck about." He stretched up and arched his back like a large cat after a nap.

Sam looked up, his emotions all over his face.

(Are you seriously gonna leave that story in a cliffhanger?)

Desmond looked like the shadow of a wild beast silhouetted in the sun. His hair was a feral mane with a beard to match. As he yawned, Sam could see a crowned tooth on the upper right of Desmond's mouth. Noticing that caused Sam to reflexively press his tongue against his own teeth. His tongue lingered on his left where he too had a crown. Desmond probably had a bout 20-25 pounds on Sam. Sam's body had been thinned out by his insufficient diet and he wondered how it was that Desmond wasn't more emaciated after his ordeal at sea.

Desmond looked down over Sam. "You got a name, mate?"

"Sam"

"Sam, Sam. Green eggs and Ham, eh? Like Dr. Seuss." Desmond teased.

Just then, it began to pour.

By his own admission, Sam was no survivalist. He had learned that on the island, but also had a strange intuitive understanding of that fact that that he couldn't completely place. It's strange the things he could remember considering he could recall virtually nothing about his life prior to being here. He can remember many trivial things, yet has no recollection of who he was, personally or professionally. If he has a family. Friends. A love life.

Of the meaningless things he could recall, he remembers having seen a few episodes of "Man vs. Wild" or "Naked and Afraid" and can remember wondering to himself how he would do if he were forced to endure in the wild. Now, having been a man in the wild, not quite naked, but definitely afraid, he'd come to realize the answer to that wonderment. Not too well.

"But maybe better than many." He thought out loud to himself.

Afterall, he's been on this island for quite some time. He's had only himself to depend on and, well, he *is* still alive. He's foraged and made fire and shelter. And aside from losing the one shoe as sacrifice to the jungle vines, isn't naked. And so long as he steers clear of the thick of the jungle, he isn't that afraid. Not too shabby.

"Sam vs Wild. Coming this spring to Discovery", he sighed.

As he faded from his thoughts back to Desmond, he started to get an uneasy feeling. He couldn't quite place it, but something about the way Desmond told the tales of his misadventure wasn't sitting right. Without warning, the rain stopped. A howl permeated the beach from the jungle and Sam's arm hairs rose like the dead.

(A monster then, eh? – Definitely!)

4. Shipwrecked

The small trolling boat slammed into the water like a cannonball that missed its mark. Desmond, his shipmate, and a bag of gear followed. Desmond was first to hurl himself into the hull. He reached out his arm and pulled his long- time friend aboard. The gear began to drift away like the final notes of a somber song. Desmond grabbed the bag and pulled it onto the boat too.

"Shit! What are we gonna do, Des?"

"Let me get my bearings, mate."

Both men were heaving and hacking a bit on swallowed sea water. The small boat rocked in a rhythmless cadence. They looked on as their fishing charter blazed a signal call to no one. The smoke rose from it like the remnants of a kamikazed naval vessel. Charred debris was scattered everywhere much of it beginning to sink. Desmond sat on the bench at the back end of the boat and opened the bag to take inventory. In it, a first aid kit. A small tarp. Some protein bars. A canteen and canteen cup. A stretch of cord. A knife- with compass. One flare gun – one flare (which Desmond quickly slid back out of sight). A deck of cards. One small net about 2' x 2'. Two waterproof matches in a cylindrical container. There were a few additional items which Sheryl must have snuck into the bag. A photograph of Sheryl and her illuminous smile that, up until recently, made Desmond swoon. A pill bottle with one pill and a note inside. The note was a gentle reminder to take the pill on time. The last item was a novel he'd been meaning to read. Even in the chaos of the moment, Desmond couldn't help himself but to notice that it seemed like part of the novel had been ripped out. A private joke he and Sheryl once shared, but now it just felt like a declaration of betrayal. Desmond laughed despite feeling pieces of himself had been ripped away in that act.

He continued to look about the boat. Within it were an oar, an additional can of water, and an emergency hand-radio. Desmond tried the trolling motor but the battery was seemingly dead. Not that it mattered, a trolling motor would be completely ineffectual against the ocean tide. Pulled from his inventorying, Desmond looked up at his mate.

"Welp, the good news is we have about two days' worth of food and water, AND we have a flare gun and emergency radio. The not as good news. No flares (he lied), a weak signal, and we're out in the middle of no man's land."

(Land?)

In all the excitement, Desmond almost forgot what brought him out in the middle of this mostly desolate stretch of ocean to begin with.

Murder.

5. The Island: Not Alone

Sam's lashes grated his eyes like gravel on a driveway. He sat against the trunk of a palm looking up as Desmond continued about the beach. In all the excitement, it took Sam a few minutes to catch onto something odd about what Desmond had told him regarding his ordeal in the ocean. Aside from that part about his prize catch. The whole thing made him uneasy, and it wasn't just because of the half-crazed look in Desmond's face. As he replayed the conversation, his uneasy feeling morphed into bewilderment. He recognized at that moment what he hadn't before. "We…" Desmond said it over and over during their conversation. "We?" Sam puzzled. "We better not muck about." "We made out ok in the drink." "We".

"My God", Sam mouthed. This guy, this Desmond, didn't seem to be alone in his mind. Someone else was on this island with them.

As this thought washed over him, Sam took a step back and adjusted his posture a bit. "Umm, Desmond," Sam started. "What are you doing?"

"No worries, chum. We're gonna take care of everything." As he spoke, he gestured to the open air next to him as if he were patting someone on the shoulder.

(How long was this guy out there?)

"Uh, alright Desmond." That's all he could muster to say. Sam watched Desmond as he erratically went back and forth along the beach edge shouting orders.

"Hurry along! That fire isn't going to build itself!"

"No, no, no! These logs will never burn. They're not seasoned yet!"

"Useless…"

And on he went, stacking wood and barking. By the end of the first day a trail of wood debris and sweat and blood was smeared from the woods' edge to a mountainous pile.

When he wasn't dragging wood over to the fire, he was running off into the woods to do God-knows-what.

"God knows," Sam thought. "But I need to see what this guy is doing."

Sam would wait for Desmond to finish his conversation with himself about how to properly place wood to make a lean-to fire and head off back into the unknown before he made a move to follow.

Desmond made his way deliberately toward Sam, knocking no one out of his way with a swat and unnecessarily helped Sam to his feet. "Sam, you watch the fire, chum. And we'll take care of the rest."

Sam couldn't speak. He stood confused as a punch-drunk boxer.

"Let's get on with it then. Stop sleeping on the job."

And off Desmond went again, mumbling into the jungle. Sam decided not to follow.

Hours went by and Desmond hadn't emerged. Sam, half out of fear and half out of necessity, kept the fire going. It was getting dark. Though Sam had been stranded and distressed for some time, he still found beauty and comfort in the way the sun rested gently on the waves across the horizon. Its shimmering reflection danced across the water with the grace and ferocity of a ballet. During these fleeting moments, Sam felt at peace. His thoughts drifted to Desmond's boat. It was a small vessel, about five to six feet in length. It was white with a blue stripe going down its belly, but the paint was faded and chipped as if it was a relic from forgotten voyages.

Sam wondered what was in the hull. Supplies? A change of clothes? A bacon double cheeseburger…? Yes, a bacon double cheeseburger with gravy fries and nice cold beer. Sam allowed his daydream to carry almost long enough that he could taste it. Then, like an oasis in the desert, it vanished. But still, there had to be something useful in that boat. After all, despite being crazy, Desmond seemed in pretty good physical shape.

Sam lifted himself and shook the sand from his shorts.

"Let's have a look." He said to no one.

6. Shipwrecked

Desmond clunked back against the aft of the rescue boat and stared at his shipmate. He hadn't yet mentioned the email he'd uncovered. Hadn't yet confronted his friend for the betrayal he committed with Desmond's wife. Hadn't yet done what he set out to do.

(At least I still have my knife)

"What the hell happened, Des?"

"Dunno, chum. She stalled out and she just went ablaze."

He wasn't completely lying about not knowing how the fire started but knew damn well why the charter stopped running. It was a well laid out plan. At least Desmond thought so when he concocted it.

7. Desmond's Past

It happened like anything life changing happens. Unexpectedly, mercilessly. It was a Saturday morning and Desmond's wife woke up earlier than usual. Desmond woke to the sound of the front door shutting just loudly and sloppily enough for him to hear the latch of a half-turned doorknob hit the strike plate.

Desmond cracked his neck and maneuvered his feet to his slippers. A roaring yawn escaping his lips. He looked over at Sheryl's side of the bed. Vacant. Naked save for his boxers, he made his way to the bedroom threshold and called out.

"Darlin'?"

"Down here." Sheryl replied against the echoing of a pot clanging.

Desmond made his way down the stairs, carelessly shuffling to the kitchen threshold. He gazed at Sheryl a moment and smiled in his thoughts. He was ever astounded and puzzled by her essence. They couldn't possibly have been created in the same image

Those weren't his words, but they perfectly defined how he viewed his wife, Sheryl. Sheryl was a professor at the local community college, and they met on campus. He wasn't a student mind you. He 'd immigrated to the states about ten years prior and was in construction. He was there building an addition to the college gymnasium. It was a story that they both loved retelling. Mostly, she liked hearing the way Desmond told it. He had a way of telling stories. Plus, she was a fool for his accent and his sort of jumbled dialect that evolved from travels in his younger days.

"We met by happenstance." He'd start. "Sheryl was walking from her last class of the day to her car and cut past the gym. Head so high up in the clouds that she tripped on the edge of my ladder and wound up with her ass in the cement. I saved her life, mate! It was still wet and was ripe to swallow her up! I swung down from my ladder and pulled her from the abyss, *Romancing the Stone* style. Her pants were wrecked, but to this day there's an imprint of that magnificent butt on the sidewalk outside the gym. I even got her to sign her name next to it. After that I followed her everywhere." He'd say with a wink.

Sheryl, bustling about, was already making Desmond coffee. She placed the coffee on the table and smiled for Desmond to sit. He did.

"Go out for a jog or something this morning, then?" He observed Sheryl's tights admiring the view.

"Just a quickie. Then I got you the paper." She pointed to the local which was resting beside him.

Desmond smiled, then mused. "You look gassed."

"A bit." she replied. "I'm gonna go hit the shower."

She leaned in and kissed Desmond a good full lipped kiss. He exhaled through a smile. As she was walking to the stairs, she glanced back to catch Desmond watching her.

"You coming?" She smiled and continued on. Desmond, utterly choiceless against his temptations, followed.

8.

Desmond found himself back on the bed alone. Sheryl, having finally made her way to the shower was washing off the morning to get ready for her Saturday afternoon class. With a stretch, Desmond seized this opportunity. He had been planning a trip for his and Sheryl's 10-year anniversary. A charter to nowhere. During which Desmond would rekindle passions with his "scorching hot" wife under the stars while the waves dance beneath their feet. Champagne, (though he was more of a bourbon guy), fresh catch, and a vow renewal. He didn't fancy himself a romantic, but this anniversary gift wasn't half bad. He already had the date set and the charter reserved. He'd whisk her off a week before their actual anniversary to throw her off the scent, which ironically was Desmond's birthday. He had already ensured that his plan would work out. The best part of it all, Desmond thought, was he planned on captaining the charter himself. He had always loved boating, and this would be his first trek in the open ocean.

Like any marriage, Desmond and Sheryl found themselves "working through" some stuff. Nothing egregious, he thought.

(Don't kid yourself, pal. It's been a rough go. That's why you are doing all of this.)

They had rebuilt what seemed like a happy marriage. They both worked hard to find back the love they had when they first met. Desmond felt that he, in particular, made great strides at becoming a better husband. Sheryl was a patient and forgiving woman, and that patience was put to the test a few times by Desmond. All that notwithstanding, Desmond and Sheryl did indeed love each other the best way they knew how, but save for an occasional spontaneous romp, they had lost that urgency to be with each other. Well, perhaps only Sheryl had.

Desmond was actually almost obsessed with his wife. He couldn't recall ever being attracted to anyone like he was to her. It truly hurt him in a way that completely fucked with his brain how the woman he loved so much, did not, at times, feel the same intense feelings of desire he felt toward her. But he really couldn't blame Sheryl, could he? Afterall, his version of love came with the occasional bout of extreme jealousy, and *other* stuff. This anniversary, Desmond hoped to spark the intense love within her once again.

That's not to say, however, that they never had sex. That fire did ignite within Sheryl from time to time, not typically in the morning though and even more rare was an invitation presented outside of on the bed. Desmond took it at face value though and left it at that.

"Darlin'?" He called out in a whispered kind of yell.

He took the silence that returned as an opening to continue his plans. He hopped out of bed to their office and opened the laptop on the desk. He hit a button to wake it from sleep mode and went to log in but was met with his wife's desktop screen. A picture of a twenty-something version of themselves at a café of sorts on a cobblestone street somewhere he couldn't recall was on the background. He noticed how few icons she kept on her desktop. Very orderly.

Rather than taking the time to switch to his account, Desmond just clicked the internet icon from hers. The browser opened with a popup which read:

"Restore last session?"

Desmond paused as if he shouldn't click yes. As if doing so would break some kind of unwritten, unspoken code of trust that, once violated, irreparably wrecks a relationship. He made an incredulous face at himself in his reflection of the screen at that ridiculous thought and clicked, "yes".

9. The Island: Cheval de Frise

As Sam slowly pushed himself from the sand his right knee popped. The aftermath of some trauma he suffered here that he can't quite recall.

(I banged it pretty hard on something)

Sam turned his head left and right, slowly and deliberately, like when people are about to tell a tasteless joke. You could see the concentration on his face as if he were trying to extend his ears outward to hear even the slightest noise indicating that he should abort his mission.

No sign of Desmond.

With the coast seemingly clear Sam began to walk toward the shipwrecked boat. He wasn't exactly sure why he was nervous or why he was sneaking over to the boat. Then again, he did know why. Desmond was definitely a bit off of his rocker. He noted earlier that it had been much farther away than he thought. And it really was. It was probably a quarter mile down the beach.

(Did I really run that far to save Desmond?)

Regardless, Sam felt compelled to get to it and retrieve that bacon cheeseburger he fantasized about earlier or, more likely, a bunch of soggy and dry-rotted remnants of once useful crap. Upon his approach, Sam started to feel a little nauseous and an ache began to linger above his right eye. Looking closely, he noticed a bunch of birds near the wreckage. They noticed him too and scattered. He also saw something even more odd. The sand near the boat was pushed up like some sort of makeshift berm. Atop the berm were wooden…

(Crosses? Are those grave markers?)

A howl pierced the silence like a bullet ricocheting around in Sam's brain. He felt his heart stop. Sam paused and the world paused around him. He crouched, suddenly feeling completely exposed, and performed a cursory scan of the tree line for Desmond…or a monster.

No sign of either.

Head down, he forged toward the berm in an erratic pattern. The slight ache above his eye rumbled more loudly intertwining with the nausea in a perfect storm. Just a few yards or so away, he looked back up. No. Not grave markers, a cheval de frise.

(Why do I know that term?)

Wooden stakes crossed over and under each other to form a barrier wall around the boat.

(Is he expecting a civil war or something?)

Sweat from his forehead had charged like calvary soldiers into his eyes stinging and blurring his capacity for thought. Carelessly, he rubbed them only to grind sand into them more deeply. His right eye fully closed from the erupting ache. He turned to see a figure silhouetted in the sun. A large, calloused hand grabbed Sam by the shoulder and spun him around. The creatures other hand raised in the air ready to pounce. Sam's head felt like it had been split. He fell to the ground with a thud. Head imprinted into the sand. As his eyes blurred, he saw a rabbit hopping in the tree line.

Then Sam blacked out.

10. Shipwrecked: A Good Plan

For now, Desmond thought to himself, the plan will have to wait. For now.

Desmond's compass was fucked. A small crack at the seam had allowed some salt water to seep in when he jumped from the charter. Having drifted for a few hours, maybe more, he'd lost all bearings.

(adrift)

Deciding that the protein bar he just finished wasn't sufficient, he began licking the inside of the wrapper, looking at his "good friend" over the top of it.

"So, what do we do, Des?"

"Fuck if I know."

"Do you know where we are?"

"Yea...Fucked." Stated matter of fact.

Desmond reached into the bag and felt the knife. He held it for a second, perhaps two, and fantasized about what he might do to the man who betrayed him and wrecked his marriage. It felt good, but he eased off and dug around until he found the deck of cards. He pulled them out with the same grip and presented them.

"Shall we?"

"Sure. We building a house or a bridge?"

"How 'bout Penang Rummy?" Desmond suggested.

"Isn't that the game where...?"

"The hands are dead. No drawing from the pile for new life." Desmond interrupted.

"Deal 'em."

As the cards flew, Desmond replayed the events of the morning, leading to the engine fire. The men had arrived at the dock around 4am. It was a twenty-footer with a large overlook deck. They boarded the boat that initially was reserved for a romantic anniversary weekend for he and Sheryl. Instead, it would be the perfect way to exact revenge, and perhaps still do a little fishing.

Desmond did a cursory check of the charter using the safety checklist which was left inside the cabin while his *best friend* loaded the gear. He used this time as an opportunity to make some modifications and rearrange some things.

- Check the hull for damage

(Ignored- she's a commercial charter)

- Check electrical system

(See above)

- Check the....

(Fuck the list. Just get to work)

Desmond moved inside the cabin looking near the steering wheel on the dash. Connected to the panel was what he was looking to *modify* first. The GPS locator for the boat. After putting the key in the ignition and turning it to the standby position, he unscrewed the panel on the dash and pulled a wire. Wrong wire. A few other lights on the panel flashed and then began to fade. They hardly seemed necessary, so he just left the wires unattached. He pulled at another wire and this time the GPS beeped and then shut down.

Next Desmond went to work on the distress radio. He wanted to make sure that he'd be able to use it again after his buddy's unfortunate accident, so he didn't cut the wires to it. He simply disconnected the hand mic and hid it in the back of one of the floor cabinets behind a bunch of blankets.

After Desmond's thorough "safety check", he removed the tether from the dock and brought up the anchor. He noticed that against the bow of the ship was a six-foot wooden boat with a trolling motor. This wasn't something typically found on a twenty foot charter, but he remembered the guy he rented it from telling him that he liked to take the charter into the bays and then drop down into the smaller boat to fish some hidden spots. A quick turn of the ignition and they were off. They headed southwest. The charter path was designated to run due north. Desmond figured he could easily make an excuse for how and why they ended up so far off course. I mean, after all, Desmond wasn't a seasoned captain or anything.

It was a good plan, but if Desmond was honest with himself, it didn't really matter. The plan needed to be just good enough to look like an accident. Convincing enough that the cops close the case and let him move on with Sheryl. Though he also wanted to leave room for Sheryl to doubt what really happened out there. It was part ego and part narcissism and completely nuts. As a failsafe if, say for example, the cops didn't believe it was an accident and began further investigating him, Desmond's backup plan was to confess his murder to Sheryl so he could see her eyes as they digest what she drove him

to do. Then before the cops could take him, he'd end it all for the both
of them.

(A good plan indeed)

11. Desmond's Past: Smoking Gun?

The browser opened a few tabs. Pinterest. Some blog about "how to spruce up your living room". A blank tab and Gmail. Pinterest was on the screen, Desmond scrolled down a bit, interested in Sheryl's interests, but it faded mid scroll. He opened the Gmail tab.

"Woah!" he said half out loud. "1408 unread emails!"

He perused. Nothing out of the ordinary. A bunch of junk mail from the graveyards of previously visited, but probably never returned to, sites. He was about to click off and stop needlessly playing detective but paused.

(What is it about having a happy life that causes trust for whom you love to wear so fickle?)

He noticed the quick links on the left-hand side. Other than the inbox, the only other tab that had a number next to it was in Drafts. Desmond couldn't help himself. He clicked on the tab and opened the email. The email wasn't addressed to anyone yet and there was nothing in the subject line. It had been drafted a few days earlier. In the body, there was just one sentence:

"yesterday was fun. ;)"

Desmond wasn't angry. He couldn't be. Save for a sudden throb in his temple, he was in a mental coma. Everything he knew and loved was wrecked in three words. Three words and a winky face.

The sound of the shower knob squeaking off shook him from his numbness back to the stinging present. He hastily attempted to leave the laptop exactly how he found it and made his way back to the bedroom. He was getting dressed as Sheryl reentered the room.

"Hey!" Desmond offered as casually as he could.

He had no idea how he wanted to play this yet. He knew that exploding on her as she entered the room would end in wreckage.

"Hey." Sheryl smiled back.

"You better hurry. Don't want to be late for class."

"Yikes! Yeah. Well, if I am and the students complain, I'll blame you for wearing me out."

"You're welcome." Desmond laughed slightly in an attempt to hide his incredulity.

Sheryl leaned over and kissed Desmond on the cheek. "Thanks." As she made her way to the door, Desmond called out.

"Darlin'?"

Sheryl turned back. "Yup."

"That was fun." He said. And he shot her a wink.

13. The Island: Ghosts

Sam woke suddenly from a nightmare that he couldn't quite remember except that he was being attacked by a...

"Werewolf?" Sam thought to himself in a whisper. Still unsure what just happened and still kind of afraid.

(Or was I attacked by a man?)

Sam slowly ran his hands over his head and arms. No signs of blood or new bruises, and aside from a slight headache and being extremely thirsty, he seemed otherwise intact.

(So, what the hell just happened?)

Sam tried to orient himself. No werewolves in sight so that was a good start. He thought for a moment and regained his bearings.

(The boat!)

As the lightbulb went on in his mind, he realized Desmond was sitting not five feet from him casually digging a small stick around in nondeliberate patterns in the sand.

"There he is!" Desmond exclaimed. "That was some performance out there."

"Huh?" Sam mustered.

"Out there on the beach. You were staggering about. Seemed almost delirious."

"Out where, Des?" Sam asked, but he knew damn well where.

Desmond smiled slightly. "You know damn well where."

Sam's face belied his surprised tone and he stammered.

"I-uh…"

"Blacked right out, ya did." Desmond interrupted. "I saw you on the beach scurrying about all hunched over like some delusional squirrel. Called out to you a few times."

"I didn't hear…" Sam trailed.

"So, I ran over to see what the hell was the matter. I patted you on the shoulder and you spun around like some deranged kook. Screamed something awful and then conked out."

Sam, still utterly confused, managed to speak somewhat coherently.

"I was on the beach, but I didn't hear you call out to me…the boat!" Sam exclaimed. "I was going to see if there was anything useful in the boat and then I saw that barricade tha-"

"Oh that! Yea. Desmond broke in. "Pretty good, ya?" A proud look in his eye.

"Pretty good? Why is there a fortified bunker around the boat, Des?" Sam's agitation and uneasiness poured through.

"For protection, of course!"

"Protection?"

"From that monster you keep mentioning, chum. Can't have some crazy island creature messing with our only seacraft, can we?" Desmond had a sarcastic, almost mocking tone.

"Okay…" Sam said meekly. "But what's in it?"

"What's in it?" Desmond repeated. "Splintered wood, dried blood, and piss bottles, mate."

"That's it?" Sam asked disbelievingly.

"That and a few ghosts." Desmond replied with a distant look.

Sam couldn't make sense of Desmond's logic. Then again, Desmond seemed bat-shit crazy.

"Anyway, mate. Best just steer clear of that boat. For your own safety." Desmond shot Sam a wink and patted him on his back.

If Sam couldn't previously find a reason to worry about Desmond before, he sure as hell found one now. Sam found himself fixated on their conversation. Particularly the change from referring to himself as *we* to *I*. He shook his head.

(What the fuck is up with this guy?)

Sam shrugged. "Ok, Desmond."

But Desmond had already gotten up and disappeared into the jungle. A loud moan echoed. The monster or his stomach? Sam wasn't sure which. However, he had an even more urgent need to find out what was in that boat. Part of him still hoping for a bacon-double cheeseburger.

14. The Island: Something Familiar

Desmond emerged from the jungle sometime later with full hands. At first, Sam thought he was carrying vines, but quickly realized Desmond had a handful of dead snakes. Holding them up and smiling proudly like a dog who unwittingly retrieved an unwanted gift for his owner, Desmond laid the snakes on a rock by the fire.

"Dinner, my good man." Desmond declared.

Sam had never been what you'd call an adventurous eater. Hell, he even would get steaks medium well done because, *that's what cooked looks like*. Never would he have guessed in a million years he'd be dining al fresco on serpents.

Sam swallowed hard. "When in Rome." He uttered aloud.

"Far way from Rome, mate." Retorted Desmond.

Sam laughed. "Yea…Thanks for the fresh catch, Des. I haven't been able to catch any of the snakes or lizards since I've been here. Not sure if it's because I'm not skilled enough or if I knew that if I did, it would mean I'd need to clean them."

"No worries." Desmond assured him. "I got us covered, mate."

Sam wasn't sure if Desmond actually knew what he was doing or if he was just crazy enough to seem like he knew, but nevertheless, Desmond laid out the snakes on a nearby rock and one by one began chopping their heads off. He pulled his knife from his hip, gave it a cursory wipe on his leg and then in one fell swoop brought the blade edge down across the base of the first snakes head. It made a kind of mushy yet crunchy sound. Then the blade clanged against the rock with a small spark. The snake head rolled from the rock like Marie

Antoinette's after facing the guillotine for treason. He followed through precisely, beheading the remaining snakes. All the while smiling oddly at Sam.

(He's having a little too much fun.)

(This is really fun.)

Desmond proceeded to strip the skin from each snake. First, he cut a little tear into the skin at the end where the heads once were. Then, he peeled the skin back, still smiling. Finally, he shoved sticks through the length of the meat and placed a few of the skewered snakes onto the fire. They made a crackling hiss. The char emanating from their flesh somehow made Sam feel a hint of nostalgia, though he couldn't place it, he could almost make out a memory through the haze. Sam began humming lightly, and then let the words of a song roll off his tongue in a whisper.

"Farewell and adieu to you…"

"Spanish ladies." Desmond added.

Sam looked up. "Jaws." He said with a smile. It's my all-time favorite movie."

"Hah. Mine too, Chiefy." Desmond smiled.

They continued to serenade the darkness until dinner was well done. The snakes weren't half bad. The men feasted and everything felt almost hopeful. Sam pulled his *toothbrush knife* from his cargo pocket and used it to pull snake bits free from between his teeth. Desmond's tone and posture, for the first time since being on the island, seemed normal to Sam. It was just then, Sam realized how utterly alone he has felt since waking up that first day. It felt good to have someone else to talk to other than himself.

As it turned out, Desmond was full of stories.

"…And this one time on the job, we were putting up gutters for this old-world Italian guy. Musta been about 70 years old. It was dead of winter, it was. And this old fella is out there in a tank top, khakis, and some house slippers. He's pulling a drag from a hand rolled cigarette just looking at us like he was warden, and we were the prison crew."

Sam leaned into Desmond's story like a little kid in a reading circle.

"I tell ya, mate, he's looking at us so intently I swore he could read our minds. Scary gent. So, we get up on the roof and of course there's four or fourteen inches of snow up there. I got the gutter up over ma shoulder and get up the ladder. Start making my way across the roof about thirty or forty feet up…and I dunno, that old codger musta been giving me the malocchio or something because the next thing I know I lost my footing on a sky light. I didn't see it because of the snow, you see, and I start tumbling ass over boots down the roof banging into whatnot as I go. I knocked my knee into something so hard it twisted me around like a crash test dummy. Gutters went flying and my crew mate starts shouting, "Noooooooooooo!""

Just then a mimicking howl sounded. Sam's ears shot back, and Desmond raised a conspicuous brow and the corner of his mouth turned up a bit into a small but discernable smile. Sam felt a flash of light go off in his head momentarily as the words from Desmond's story replayed. He pictured himself in Desmond's place, tumbling off the edge. He could almost smell the snow.

"Where was I? Oh, yea. So, he shouts, "Noooooooo!" and I'm tumbling off the roof grabbing at anything like a cat on a ledge trying escape that old kook's curse. Mid tumble everything slowed down for a second and I can remember seeing birds scatter from a nearby tree in a ballet of chaos…Anyway, I'm just about at the end now and my mate lays down in a lunge to try to catch me, cliffhanger style, but I was out of reach. In a last-ditch effort, I pulled my hammer from my belt and jabbed the claw end into the roof. It caught one of the last rows of shingles just in time to stop my free fall. Feet dangling off the edge like a dare."

"I pull myself back up and get to my knees and instinctually look down at my would be demise and there I see that old nutter standing in my landing zone in his tank just looking up at me, still pulling a drag from his cigarette. I don't want to catch his eye, but I do…Then, he just blows the smoke from the side of his mouth like a truck exhaust, turns, and goes back into the house without a word. I tell ya, he was the scariest thing about the whole ordeal."

Sam felt the ache in his knee where he had earlier. Perhaps a sympathy pain from Desmond's tale. Still, something about that story seemed familiar. Like something from an old Chevy Chase movie or something. He couldn't quite place it. Regardless, he felt normal for a moment. No longer alone. Almost like he was a young scout, sitting around telling stories with his fellow campers. Only thing missing was some marsh mellows.

15. The Island: Hunters and Prey

The next morning, Sam woke up surprisingly refreshed. The protein from the snakes was a charge of energy and strength he'd been missing since his first day on the island. Perhaps, he thought, he misjudged Desmond. Sure, he is quirky, a little crazy even, but he is resourceful and actually a pretty good conversationalist when he isn't ranting to himself. Besides, Sam wasn't completely convinced that he wasn't a bit crazy himself. Afterall, he wasn't certain just how long he'd been on the island. And life before his arrival was an apparition. Nonetheless, Sam recognized the value in Desmond's arrival and thought it'd be helpful to learn how to hunt for food.

Desmond, of course, was already up and off somewhere. Sam began getting himself together when Desmond appeared.

"Alright then." Desmond quipped. "Up and at'em."

"Hey, Desmond." Sam began. "Thanks for the snake."

"No worries."

"I was thinking. I should learn how to catch snakes too, ya know? Can you teach me?"

"Aha!" Desmond exclaimed. "Want me to teach you the kill, eh? Then you can do away with old Desmond. That it?"

Sam looked quizzically.

"Just teasing, mate. Of course, I'll show ya. But snakes are Easy. Let's go proper hunting. Maybe we'll catch us a monster."

Sam laughed nervously.

"You'll be alright mate. I'll make sure the jungle doesn't eat your shoes."

(But who will make sure a monster doesn't catch and eat us)

"What do you think is out there?"

"Well, mate. I'm pretty sure there are monkeys way in there, but we don't wanna mess with them. Even if we did manage to bag one of them without it ripping our faces off, their riddled with parasites and other nasty buggers."

"Yea, pretty sure I'm not eating monkey."

"There's definitely some other critters out there. I've heard them scurrying around. I'm sure we'll find something. Lemme show you a few things before we head out."

Sam was impressed by how much Desmond knew about primitive hunting. Though in all honesty he wouldn't be able to tell the difference if Desmond was making it all up as he went. They made a set of spears and gathered some ropes to possibly set some snares in various spots. After Desmond's seminar in the sand, the men moved off into the jungle to see what they could catch.

Sam followed fairly closely behind Desmond as they made their way into the thick of the jungle. Uneasiness swelled in Sam's stomach. Acid was bubbling to the point where he could taste it in his throat and yet, a part of him was excited. He finally felt like he was doing something better than simply surviving.

Stepping carefully to avoid twigs that would readily give up their position, they moved along the small, trailed paths where the underbrush had been matted down by the movement of the jungle's natural inhabitants. Perhaps some kind of medium sized cat or boar.

Though it was mid-morning and full sun on the beach, under the canopy of the trees, the light fought with the foliage to penetrate the landscape causing a kaleidoscope of rays to cascade down in a patternless fashion. It gave the jungle an eerie feeling. Shadows shifted and bent around the plant life making shapes that played tricks on the mind.

Desmond crouched down and held his hand up in a fist like some NCO in a Vietnam war movie. Sam crouched behind. Eyes wide open scanning the landscape with no idea what he was looking for. After a minute or so of silent crouching, Sam could hear what must have made Desmond stop. There was rustling in the brush nearby. First, in front of them about five yards or so. Whatever it was sounded as if it were moving away. Desmond sprung up and waved his hand to suggest they follow it.

Both men were moving quickly. There quietness gave way to a more sounded cadence. Whatever it was that they were chasing ran swiftly, a spattering of broken twigs in its wake. The men were hustling now, pausing here and there to try to make out the movement of whatever they were stalking. A branch snapping to their left sent Desmond bounding of the path through the brush. Leaving behind him only the trailing reverberation of his own voice calling out for Sam to follow.

Sam obliged, hurtling himself into the heavy undergrowth. In doing so, Sam stumbled off balance and landed on his side into a small boggy patch. Snaps and creeks were abundant in the surrounding area now. The apparent sound of fleeing jungle creatures.

He regained his footing and continued after Desmond, but he lost sight of him around a bend of trees.

"Shit! Desmond hold up!" Sam cried out vainly.

Sam's head was on a pivot as he shuffled about, trying to gain his bearings. The voices of the jungle began to flex. All around him now were the buzzings and bellows of unseen monsters. He was spinning now. From the corner of his eye, he caught a glimpse of something scampering through a bush, disappearing from sight too quickly to identify. To his other side, a creature darted through the thick vines, heard but not seen at all. In every direction the jungle looked exactly the same. Finally, he chose a path and began walking slowly along its edge. On the sides lay tree trunks and branches with the haphazardness of nature. Almost tiptoeing, Sam became astutely aware of his heaving breaths.

"I'm gonna fucking die in this jungle." He murmured to no one.

Just then Sam felt it. The powerful grip of something pulling him down. Trying to drag him down into the jungle. One paw or hand over his mouth, muffling his screams, another wrapped around his torso. In a panic, Sam began kicking trying to break free from what he guessed was a monster about to feed on him, but he was unable. He was dragged down under a nestle of branches. Eyes closed, he prepared for the worst.

"Mate! Mate! It's me" Desmond shouted in a whisper.

"What the fuck are you doing?" Sam shouted back, not so much in a whisper.

"Shhhhh." Desmond hushed Sam and, with his eyes, pointed out into the jungle. "Look! You see it?"

Sam squinted and looked in the direction which Desmond was faced. At first, Sam didn't see anything, but then, it revealed itself. Just to the other side of the path on an elevated area of the jungle sat a small, patchy rabbit.

"You see it, right mate?

"I see it."

"Good. I thought I was going crazy there." Desmond said good naturedly.

"Let's get it." Sam challenged.

"We will, mate. We'll get her, just not today."

Sam looked over at Desmond.

"Rabbits are clever little rascals. We'll have to come back out when she's not in sight and set up some traps."

Sam didn't relish the idea of coming back into the jungle despite the whole thing being his idea. Either way, he knew Desmond was right. No use trying to catch an animal that knows its being watched. Besides, it was getting late, and they needed to find their way back to camp before the real monsters came out.

The trek wasn't a total waste. On the way back, Desmond snagged them a few more snakes. Sam even caught one with his own spear. A successful hunt in Sam's estimation. They feasted in similar fashion to the previous night. Perhaps everything would be okay after all.

16. Shipwrecked: MAD

The boat had been rocking in the water like a song you're tired of hearing for what Desmond estimated to be a few days. Floating about in helter-skelter. Desmond and his old friend were slouched on opposite ends. He turned his shirt into a do-rag which he soaked in the ocean before wrapping around his head. His mate fashioned the small tarp into a canopy. He lay under it with his eyes closed against the heat. Desmond began whistling an old sea shanty through cracked lips. The air felt like razors on his pallet. Swigging back a shot from the canteen, he began to look around.

"Water, water everywhere…ah, fuck it." Desmond decided. He stood up, looked his mate in the eye, raised his hands up, and jumped into the ocean cannonball style.

The water tidal waved into the boat soaking the canopy and its inhabitant.

A surrender from inside. "What the hell?"

Desmond emerged from the depths proud to see his cannonball hit its target. Beard glistening in small explosions like a 4th of July finale. The position of the sun indicated that it was sometime in the midafternoon and the salt in the air was palpable. He seemed to float up toward the boat's edge and spit water from his mouth like a marble depiction of Zeus, which also hit its target.

"Ok, ok, I'm up."

Desmond pulled himself back up onto the boat with a groan. His knee protested the maneuver.

"Alright then. Let's say we try to catch us some grub." Desmond began digging into the bag. He pulled out the compass and the length of cord. And began examining the compass.

"Think I can fashion some sort of lure with this."

He held it up. Shiny and gold. A gift to him from Sheryl for their anniversary. It was a replica of a British Naval fleet design. Within it was an ornate azimuth ring with detailed etchings and a customized needle which had a small ship engraved into it. The outside was personalized with the acronym, "MAD" and a heart shape. The acronym, love letters between them.

"Merry Always, Darlin'." Desmond read aloud.

17. The First Few Days on the Island

Sam was ripped from his dreams. He rubbed his eyes. They burned like acreage in the California forests. A loud cracking sound followed by a tree falling through the limbs of other trees like a frontline soldier in the crosshairs of sniper fire caused Sam to duck instinctually, uncertain of where it might land. The ground shook behind him and he jolted around. He was confronted by think foliage. A panic set in quick like when a child loses sight of his mother in a department store.

"Where the hell?" he murmured.

Groggily, Sam got to his feet despite the protest of his knee which was bruised and a bit swollen. Looking around he became immediately aware of his situation. On the near shoreline, Sam could see some debris and a once seaworthy boat.

All at once, the events that directly preceded his awakening flashed before his eyes like they say life does on your way to Heaven…or Hell. Only, the flashes weren't much more than blurred images overlapping like double exposed photos. Trying to focus in on any one of them proved fruitless. Sharp pain on his brow caused him to wince. He pinched his nose in an attempt to subside it and peered over his knuckles.

Sam looked to the wreck and made a few limped steps toward it but stopped himself. It was in opposition of all logic, not checking the wreckage. Yet, Sam quickly developed an inner conflict over the thought. The pain was piercing his head like needles at the hands of a sadistic acupuncturist. Again, he grabbed the bridge of his nose and closed his eyes attempting to will it away. He stood frozen for a moment, like his body was rebooting. The hot stinging of his body's ailments was in direct juxtaposition to the cool breeze drifting off of the waves. His ears were ringing, clashing with the melodic sounds of some unrecognizable birds in the tree line. After a cursory scan across his periphery, Sam tried to regain his bearings and headed toward their calls.

Just within the tree line, the soundtrack of the island switched from serene waves and rustling palms to echoes of creatures unseen. Overcrowded with chatter, even the trees were whispering ominously as if taking underhanded bets on Sam's next moves. Slowly, Sam stepped through the limbs and creepers. The mist permeated the air with a blend of vegetation. Wind gusted through the trees in popping bursts. The branches perpetual shifts played games with the shadows below. Sam's eyes darted around trying to discern the innocuous ones from any potential threats. Even at midday, it felt more like dusk under the huge canopy of greens.

Despite the thick underbrush, there seemed to be few areas of path, or at least matted down lengths of land.

"Lions and tigers and…oh my." he thought out loud to himself.

Still, Sam couldn't help but wonder what monsters might be out there waiting for him to get within striking distance. Looking back, he realized he had already gone in about 40 or 50 yards. He began to hum a song he didn't quite know to a memory that didn't feel like his own. A date. He could almost see her face and he caught a glimpse of perfume in this memory. He lingered into it hoping to drift from his present to live out the rest of his days inside that blur when, suddenly, his focus was redirected.

"CRACK!"

The snaps of branches and whirling rustles of earth were suddenly all around him like tornadoes. He stammered and his head jolted around on a pivot trying to capture whoever, whatever was closing in. Heart pounding like a battle drum, ricocheting through his insides and reverberating in his ears. Even louder still was the rustling on the ground. He swiveled around catching a shadow darting behind a tree. And then another. With each passing shadow the trees seemingly whispered, "look over here."

With the shadows choking the air around him, Sam began to panic. His eyes shifted trying to find a line of sight back to the shoreline. In one swift movement he began to run, but something grabbed his leg and pulled him to the ground. He began to swing downward blindly, violently toward his legs in hysteria attempting to free himself from the whatever it was. Demons seemingly trying to pull him into the depths of hell. He attempted like hell to kick free, but the grasp of unseen demons' tentacles only seemed to tighten with each increasingly labored breath. They had him, but not demons. Vines. Vines had him trapped. Entangling him like an unhealthy relationship. His panic subsided in a rush of embarrassment and confusion. He felt utterly silly and impotent. He sat just long enough to catch his breath again, and then calmy begin to untangle his legs. Kicking free, he could see a shadow barreling toward him. Just as quickly as he could stand, he was knocked back to the ground his head slamming down, bouncing off the surface. His vision hazed over, and a strong scent invaded his nostrils. It was familiar, perhaps pepper. Then everything went dark.

■ ■

Sam woke up alone in a gasp and jolted upward from a vivid dream that quickly began to blur. A cursory scan of his surroundings alerted him to the fact that he was back on the edge of the tree line at the beach, not where he was attacked.

(Was I attacked?)

Sam wasn't sure what happened. He wasn't even sure how much time had passed since he blacked out in the jungle. Hours? Days? His stomach growled ferociously making him think it was the latter. He reached down to his calves, still feeling the pull of the vines. Glancing over his knees, he realized he was missing one of his shoes. All in all, it was a pretty rough first trek in the jungle. Sam stood and stretched. His head and body whimpered, and his muscles held tight in obstinance. His attention was brought to the shoreline by a flock of birds. His boat was gone. Sam started in its previous direction but recognized the futility of it and stopped. It seemed impossible to gain focus on anything. He still couldn't recall how the hell he got there.

(It must have drifted with the tide or something.)

Regardless, Sam decided he must get his *shit* together and figure out what he was going to do. Venturing back into the jungle was out for now, though he would have to confront the dodgy situation that occurred and make some sense of it at some point. First thing's first. Sam began walking the tree line in search of some food. There had to be some coconuts or berries or melons or something on the outer edge of the jungle. He did note that there seemed to be plenty of fruit on the jungle floor.

The rest of Sam's day was spent gathering food and branches. As he worked bringing them back to the stretch of beach that he chose to call home he tried to reconcile with the idea that he may be on the island for a while, and with the fact that he had very little idea how he got there. He was exhausted and straining his brain trying to recall only seemed to make him feel worse.

"I suppose," he thought, "not remembering could be a good thing. If I were a great man, the memories of my life would torment me. If I were a murderer or something, they'd likely haunt me."

■ ■

By the next day on the island, volcanic heat emanated from Sam's crusted lips and was a blistering warning that he needed to find a water source soon. Either that or perform some kind of Incan sacrifice. Sam rose from his hasty shelter, a bit dizzy from everything, and continued to travel the route he had the previous day along the edges of the jungle in search of water.

It's an amazing and incredibly troubling fact that no matter where you find yourself on this Earth you will come across human refuse. Never mind if the place you happen to find yourself is on a seemingly otherwise deserted island in the middle of God knows where, you will still invariably find a treasure trove of crap washed up from some distant land where gluttony and carelessness reside.

This island was no exception to that truth. As Sam walked, he stumbled upon a pile of seaweed and whatnot. Visible within the tangle, was a large plastic bottle. Sam rummaged it out of the seaweed, and it was in fact a two-liter soda bottle, completely intact. Further rummaging produced a rusty tin can (with the jagged top still clinging on for dear life), a flip flop, and a toothbrush. At one end it was broken and jagged. At the other, a few misshapen bristles clinging to its head like the beginnings of a beard on a pubescent teenager.

"Score!" Sam yelled as he held the flip flop in the air as if shoving it in the face of God. He bent down and put it on. Of course, it was the wrong size and for the opposite foot, but it was better than nothing. The soda bottle and tin can would certainly come in handy, he figured, if he found some potable water before he died of dehydration. He wasn't sure what he'd do with the toothbrush, but held onto it, nonetheless.

Sam continued along the jungle's edge where he reached a sharp bend in the tree line. At that point, the island took on an odd, almost unnatural shape. Sam hadn't noticed it while walking, but he had been going up a very slight incline. Where he now stood was slightly elevated from the ocean. About fifteen feet from where he stood there was a drop off leading to it. To the left were still the trees and, in front of him, lay a huge patch of flat land. Matted down trees and brush, flattened out as if they had been crushed by the foot of a giant. At the center of the giant *footprint*, Sam could see a pool of water. A shot of adrenaline and hope washed through his veins. Despite his newfound surge of energy, he moved gingerly toward it as to not lose his other shoe in the tangles of brush. The last few feet to the water were clear and Sam moved quickly to it. He fell to his knees and threw his lips to the water. He slurped an uncounted amount of huge gulps from the pond without regard to what microscopic horrors might be swimming within.

With a sigh, Sam tilted his head back, eyes closed in utopic relief. Then he began to violently regurgitate what he had taken in. He had drunk too much too fast. Slowly, he reopened his eyes and took a closer look at the water. It was pretty clear and didn't seem to have any algae or other muck floating in it. That was encouraging as Sam became suddenly aware that he may have even worse issues than some vomit later on if the water was indeed infested with bacteria. The diameter of the pond was roughly thirty to fifty feet and water was feeding into it in a cascade of ledges. From now on, Sam decided, the water fall is where he'd get his water. The water at the fall was likely to be much safer than that in the plunge pool. With the water problem solved, Sam knew that next he'd have to move camp a bit closer and build a shelter.

There was some rustling nearby. Some branches snapped, seemingly under the feet of a native inhabitant of the island. Sam became astutely aware that if this water source is his best option, then it was also likely the best option for whatever other creatures are stranded on this rock. This could prove to be a problem depending upon the prowess of the yet unseen animals.

Sam spent the next hour or so dragging his stuff over to his newly selected camp site. He was about three-quarters of the way back with the remainder of the tangibles when he started to break out into a cold sweat. It was immediate and perfuse sending a shiver down his arms and legs. His stomach began to groan like a scolded housecat, and then tightened as if being gripped by an invisible giant's hand. Sam doubled over mid stride, his bag falling from his back to the sand in a thud. He followed it to his knees. Arms thrown across his waist in a hug that offered no consolation. He felt like he was going to erupt in devastation from everywhere like a stratovolcano.

Weakly, Sam found his footing and staggered his way back to his new campsite. Nothing was set up yet. His hasty shelter was laid out on the sand. Rummaging in his bag, he pulled out the soda bottle filled with water from the fall and took a swig. As the water hit his lips, so too did the realization hit his brain that this sudden onset of pain and illness must have been from drinking from the plunge pool. He threw the soda bottle mindlessly, it tumbled and the remainder of the clean water he had collected spilled out. He fell to a seated position with a thud and began convulsing in the sand. Involuntarily, tears fell from his eyes. He closed them and began to rock himself in the fetal position, clutching his knees to his chest like an abandoned child. He was on an island. He was alone. He had no idea how he got there. He couldn't remember who he was. These are the thoughts that bombarded his mind. He began to fall unconscious in the edge of the jungle. As his eyes shuttered closed. He heard nearby rustling in the trees. Sam didn't have the strength to stay conscious long enough to see what was coming for him. He fell back, flat into the sand. Arms stretched out

From deep within his unconscious state, Sam dreamt.

■ ■

Walking in the night down a modestly lit stone street, Sam felt a strong sense of calm. It was warm despite the dampness of a recent rain on the ground. He wasn't alone. There was someone else there with him. A woman. She smiled up at him as the strolled, her arm around his. Her smile was a source of light from which Sam could clearly see his immediate surroundings. The buildings were old, but not run down. Each housed a store of some sort with slightly out of focus yet attractive window displays. Dim lanterns were in a row along their path and there was noise from other pedestrians as they passed by. Sam and the woman paused their stride and she pointed out something in a nearby windowfront. She began to speak to him in a tone that suggested comfortability and perhaps a hint of flirtiness. Her voice was angelic, songs of a siren on the sea, but her words were mangled like an old wooden vessel rotting on the seabed. Whatever it was that she was pointing out to him was glared out of vision. He squinted in the way that for some reason people do when they are *really* trying to see something. Despite his efforts, only their reflection was visible in the window.

Sam became anxious. The woman, still talking to him about whatever it was in the store, began to utter sounds more erratically. Her words were becoming sharp and off-pitch, stinging his brain like a misfired synapse. Every syllable spit from the edge of her tongue ricocheted more violently than the previous until Sam felt as though he were under attack. He began to impulsively flinch, ducking the barrage. His heartbeat echoed loudly reverberating the windowpane causing their reflections to tremble in waves. Suddenly, time stopped. All noise stopped. All motion. Stopped. Just long enough for Sam to breathe in one shivered breath. All at once, gravity began to come undone. He could feel the shift. Droplets were lifting from the puddles beneath their feet. Slowly at first, each, one by one, raising like the dead to his eye level and pausing just long enough for him to see his own uncertain face staring back at him a million times over. Each then whirling upward toward the sky before exploding into the clouds. The woman too appeared to be levitating from the ground. Or was gravity pulling Sam down into the Earth? The beautiful woman's mouth began to transform into a hideously wide gape, in which laid rows of jagged teeth. Her head swelled like an overexpanded balloon, widening her face, and exaggerating her nefarious smile. Her eyes shimmered black with an endless depth. In them, again, he saw his reflection over and over and over like a funhouse mirror. Sam felt as if he were drowning and couldn't break free. He started to flail about. His arms heavier and heavier from the weight of his own fear. In that moment, the woman's head plunged forward toward Sam and with her razor sharp teeth, she bit his head clean off.

Sam's vision floated free into the air above the street. Now weightless, a strange relief washed over him. He saw his own headless body. Arms still floundering. He could feel his head sliding down the throat of the hideous she beast before him. Tumbling to its stomach with a thud before everything went black.

Sam found himself sitting in the darkness. Still entrenched in a nightmare. A small light in the distance broke the silence of the eternal blackness surrounding him. Sam searched around his head and body with his hands to feel that everything was intact. It was. The glow from the distant glow began to radiate further outward allowing just enough light for Sam to see shapes. A short distance in front of him sat a silhouetted shape of a motionless man. He couldn't see his face, but Sam had an instant feeling of familiarity which made him uneasy. The seat upon which Sam sat began to sway gently. Looking down over his left shoulder he could see the ground moving beneath him. Not ground, liquid. Strange water. Dark and thick. Spots of bubbles popped asynchronously at the surface. Sam was in a boat. A boat made of paper. Upon closer inspection, Sam noticed that the paper had typing all over it as if they were pages from a novel. Looking back up to the figure seated across from him, he could now make out its face. It was him. The other figure in the boat had Sam's face and frozen on it was an eerie smile. Its eyes were wide open like a realization of truth. Sam felt no such realization. He waved his hand in front of its face. It did not blink. It did not move.

As surreal as all of this was, Sam was more bewildered than he was frightened. He reached down to touch the hull of the paper boat. It was soggy and ready to fall apart. When he placed his hand on one of the typed words, *sand,* it lifted from the paper and all at once crumbled into a physical manifestation of itself, falling to the liquid beneath the boat causing a sizzle upon impact. Suddenly, as if they were interstellar aircraft attempting to flee a planet on the verge of annihilation, the words began to lift from the boat in a rush and fly off into the darkness. With each fleeing word, the boat began to sink. Whatever Sam was feeling previously, he was now terrified. Panic set in and he began to look around frantically for an escape. There was nothing in sight and no word that flew from the boat was large enough to carry him. Sam's seemingly lifeless doppelganger from the other side of the paper boat jumped up from a petrified state and began dancing some crazy looking jig reminiscent of old cartoon skeletons in a black and white Halloween special. It began loudly mumbling some out of tune song which echoed off the emptiness like memories. Then, just as suddenly as it began its routine, the figure dropped back down to the seat like a discarded marionette puppet. Eerie smile and all.

The boat was barely treading the liquid. Sam's hand brushed against the liquids surface. When he pulled his hand up to his face, what he saw caused him to gasp. The liquid into which he was sinking, was blood. It dripped from his hand boldly like an accusation as the boat made its final descent. He looked through his bloodied fingers at his doppelganger, its eyes were bleeding, and it was murmuring in his direction revealing something Sam couldn't quite make out. Finally, they were submerged to their necks for what felt like an eternity. The figure winked. Then, he was drowned.

■ ■

Sam awoke from this nightmare in a gasp. He heaved rapidly to catch his breath and darted upward to a seated position to take in his surroundings. The sun was beating down on him in oppressively and his mouth was crusted with dried vomit, but he was ok. No man-eating monster stood before him. No blood ocean rippled beneath him. Sam was not yet swallowed. Not yet dead. He was alive and was utterly alone.

18. Desmond's Past: Wrecked

Desmond read somewhere once that you should always wait a few minutes after someone leaves before you do something you don't want them to see just in case they forgot something and double back. Desmond didn't really care. As soon as he heard Sheryl close the front door, he sprung from the bed and began tossing the bedroom like a drill sergeant during a barracks inspection.

"Who the fuck was that email to?" He wondered aloud as he made his way to her side of the bed.

He nearly pulled the nightstand drawer from its slides and began rummaging back and forth through its contents.

"Fuckin' mess…" Desmond wasn't sure if he was talking about the drawer or his current situation.

He pushed things around with little rhyme or reason as if whatever incriminating evidence may be inside would jump out at him in surrender, but nothing inside seemed to scream, "I'M CHEATING ON YOU!" He moved on and about the room. His focus landed on the small mesh wire garbage pail. Wadded tissue blossomed over the rim and tangled over the edges. He gingerly moved a few aside looking for…a used condom? A receipt? Reaching around a bit more his hand brushed across something gooey. Gum.

Desmond's mind was chewed into a mush. He went across the hall, back into the office. Emptiness where the laptop once was.

"How could you fuckin' do this to me?" his vision slightly blurred through a tear.

"You wrecked us."

19. Shipwrecked: Meditation

"Merry always, darlin'." Desmond thought, and then smashed the compass down bludgeoning it hard against the inside of the hull. It broke apart in his hands. Irony sat listlessly on his mind.

He grabbed the spring and the needle and began working them to shape.

(This needle is way too thin and flimsy to work as a hook in an ocean tide.)

"Fuck off." Desmond whispered to no one as he worked.

"Des?" Asked watchful eyes from across the boat.

"Yea."

"Not that I doubt your seaward prowess or anything, but uh…what are we gonna use as bait?"

Desmond chuckled lowly. "Gonna have to carve you up a bit, chum."

Watchful eyes widened with a chuckle of their own. "No, seriously."

"Well." Desmond considered. "This aughta do it!"

He grabbed one of the protein bars and broke off a chunk, Then, without missing a beat, he rolled it against a gash near his knee. He held up the blood-soaked health snack with a kind of dopey smile like he was James Wilson Marshall holding up a gold nugget at Sutter's Mill.

Watchful eyes cringed as Desmond baited the hook and ran the cord through his hands in a bundle. The weight shifted hard in the boat as he cast his line.

The sun was at its highest point now and both men were feeling the drain of dehydration. The water was long gone, and it hadn't rained. Desmond steadily watched for his prize catch. The line lay limply on the surface. The effects of the sun were blatant on Desmond's skin. His shoulders blistered and torn like an old leather couch in a cat-lady's apartment. His mate, his one-time best friend, a little less worse for the wear. For now. The tarp had provided decent shelter and Desmond seemed to prefer to be without it.

Desmond's mind drifted back to his plan. He hadn't forgotten why they were out there and he damn sure wasn't going to withdraw from it. Still, all this time adrift made the act a bit more sinister. It was one thing when everything was going step by step. The buildup to the moment when he would confront his wife's coconspirator. The inevitable denial of it all. The swell of rage and adrenaline washing over him like a tidal wave. All culminating in one self-satisfying, and self-justifying act of vengeance.

It would have been an accident of course. The story has been told many times. Two buddies go out on a fishing trip. They get a bit lost and one of them doesn't make it back. The details of the story vary. Sometimes the person lost at sea is said to be a hero who risked his life to save those ultimately rescued. Other times, it's a simple slip and fall into the water never to surface again. Desmond hadn't actually planned out the full details of his story upon rescue. He just knew he would be coming home alone. He had laid out a few options for the actual act, though they were limited as well. Initially, Desmond had considered bringing a gun to finish the job. That idea, he decided, was a bad one just in case his would be rescuers happened to recover a body. No way to explain a chest full of bullet wounds. Some ideas that made the final cut included making his buddy walk the proverbial plank. He also considered a simple shove at the right moment over the side or, even better, off the back of the boat. Then, somehow throttling the engine, perhaps mangling the body in the process, and letting sharks take care of the rest. The idea of a finale including a shark frenzy was part of every scenario. What better way to complete the act than to watch a bunch of blood thirsty sharks tear his enemy apart?

(If only I had a beer)

Ultimately, Desmond decided that he wanted the murder he committed to be a bit more up close and personal. Afterall, his wife spent plenty of time getting up close and personal, why shouldn't he? After confronting the man who wrecked his marriage, he would bludgeon him with a small club he had brought. It was not a club, but a small baseball bat which he had gotten during "bat day" at a game that, ironically, his buddy had taken him to a few years back. Desmond didn't intend on killing his friend with the bat, just incapacitate him enough to get the better of him. Desmond wanted to finish the job in a more sinister way. He'd strangle his buddy to death. He'd strangle him and, as he did, he would hum his wedding song.

(Beautiful)

Desmond smiled and began to play out his return. He envisioned sitting on the rescue vessel with shivers from the rough seas. Steam emanating from the water as the moon rippled across the horizon. Some sort of rough blanket over his shoulders. A cup of coffee in his hands while crewmen call for maydays and ask him about the ordeal with a hand on his shoulder. The first steps onto the dock. Boards creaking under his feet. A light post silhouetting a news reporter waiting eagerly to get the scoop regarding his harrowing escape from an endless sea. The wind blowing Sheryl's hair as she stood at the edge of the port tightly holding a cardigan around her to shield her from the cool night air. He pictured the redness in her eyes and paused his movie. He couldn't decide what combination of feelings he wanted to see most prominently in them. Guilt? Regret? Thankfulness? Fear?

A splash broke him from his fantasy.

20. The Island: Follow the Rabbit

The night of the hunt, Sam had a terribly strange dream. He was drifting on a boat over pitch blackness which somehow felt empty but was bubbling in spouts around him. The bubbles splattered droplets of blackness into the air, a few of which landed on him and the boat, singeing the wood and his body as they hit. From the distance, walking across the plain of the blackness, there was a rabbit. As it neared, Sam noticed its hair was caked in blood and within its mouth was the ripped open body of a headless snake. The rabbit looked at Sam and Sam could read its thoughts. It was telling him to follow it into the blackness. Sam felt compelled. He stepped off the edge of the boat, but when he did, he didn't land. Instead, he just fell through the blackness, endlessly, until he woke up.

Sam gasped and jolted upward from his dream. He couldn't recall what it was about. Something about a rabbit and falling. The sun was already in his eye and the embers from last night's fire were dancing in his nostrils. A few heaving breaths. Sam tried to remember what had him in such a panic just then, but it alluded him. Looking down, he saw a winky face in the sand made of snake heads.

"Jesus!" Sam exclaimed. "Fucking psycho." He shook his head.

(Desmond's attempt to be cute? Or something more sinister at play? What's with the wink?)

All of this. The island. The jungle. The Monster within. The boat. The explosive headaches and Desmond. It all felt like a demented nightmare. His time here had been muddled much like his dream. He was losing touch with his reality. It didn't help that he still couldn't quite remember things before he woke up on the island for the first time. Vivid dreams that have blended into shapeless, jumbled drifts.

Sam slowly stood and backed away from the Medusa's wink and brushed himself free of the sand. He began walking across the beach. As he crossed, a few dolphins leapt up from just beyond the crashing tide and danced along the sea ridge. Pausing to admire them, he imagined they were mermaids. Naked sirens calling for him to join them in their seductive dance. Entranced, Sam lost himself in the moment. He imagined himself on a boat heading toward them. He thought about coasting up to them and began to play out some strange folklore. He lingered in that thought for a bit, but the dolphins shook free from the captivity of his fantasy and splashed back into the water below leaving Sam in his imaginary vessel.

"The Boat!" He jolted as he remembered his mission.

His eyes shifted to where the boat had been, just inside the hasty berm that Desmond put up, but it was gone. Sam sprinted toward the berm, stumbling over his own feet in the sand. As he got closer, he could see drag lines where the boat had been, stopping him dead in his tracks. The drag lines went into the water and disappeared. So too did Sam's hope. His heart dropped. Even if the boat was wrecked and offered no real chance for rescue, it made him feel as though he weren't forgotten on this Godforsaken Island. Now, he felt condemned to purgatory.

"I can't even remember how the fuck I got here!" Sam exclaimed in agony. Pain rippled like waves across his forehead.

"Where the fuck are you, Desmond? DESMOOOOOOOOND?! You son-of-a-bitch!" Almost deliriously, Sam began cursing and screaming in circles to no one, but the echoes of his own voice bouncing off of the jungle.

21. The Island: What Good is a Boat Anyway?

Desmond emerged boisterously from the jungle a few hours later. Naked and covered in blood and dirt. He was grinning crazily from ear to ear in either excitement or delusion. He trod toward Sam, eyes wide as the shoreline. His arms were swinging pendulums splattering blood back and forth as he moved. Sam instinctually got into a slight defensive stance.

Sam started to mutter. "Desmond what the fu-"

"Mate, you gotta see this!" Desmond interrupted. As he spoke, he flailed his arm upward. Blood rolled down his hand and splashed a trail across the sand. He continued in a ramble.

"I was out scouting about the jungle lookin' for supplies and food and whatnot and, I mean, I'm in the thick of it out there. Climbing muddy hills and dancing through vines. I got about a mile or so in, pulling myself up to the top of this ridge out thataways by the trunk of a palm. Then outta the trees came a howl." He paused for a breath.

"A howl?" Sam was able to mutter in.

"A howl. Some ungodly bellow. I out right never heard such a thing. It damn near scared me right out of my trunks up the ridge. Anyway, I figured if it's my time so be it. No way out from where I was but up the ridge. Rustling was all around me, but there was nothing there except me. Until..." He trailed for a second and looked back toward the jungle with one of those 1000-yard stares common to war veterans. Sam shifted his weight which broke Desmond from his episode. Desmond turned back toward Sam, tilted his head slightly to the right and queried.

"You think I'm fuckin' nuts, eh? Coo-coo??"

Sam sighed. "I, uh."

Desmond curled one side of his mouth up and patted Sam firmly on the shoulder.

"Perhaps I am a bit wacko, eh? There, see? A crazy person, a real nutbag...would protest. So maybe I'm only have crazed. Now, where was I? Ah, yes. The howling monsters. I was up there all alone. Surrounded."

The juxtaposition in Desmond's words gave Sam a familiar feeling of his own encounters in the jungle.

"I got up on my feet at the top of the ridge pulled out my knife." He pulled out his knife in demonstration. "And spun around ready to gut whatever was closing in on me...Then, it just stopped. The noises. The rustling. They were all apparitions. It was just me, standing there, knuckles white in a cold sweat."

Desmond laughed a hearty laugh. Then continued through a pant.

"It was just me...Well, me and George."

"George?" Sam asked to himself.

"George?" Sam asked out loud.

"Yea, mate. Come with me. You're gonna wanna see this."

"Des." Sam interjected. "What's with all the blood? And your clothes? I mean, what the hell, man?"

"Blood? Clothes?" Desmond replied rhetorically. "Just a little aftermath from my battle at bunker hill is all. Never mind that. Come on."

Everything about this made Sam feel uneasy. Where he had felt like he was in a repeating episode of the *Twilight Zone*, it was beginning to be more like *Tales from the Crypt*. The madness of Desmond's story after his blood-soaked birth emerging from the tree line caused him to forget about the missing boat. Despite all of it, Sam was compelled to follow Desmond into the jungle. But not before he told him to put some clothes on.

Desmond led Sam through the jungle back to where his surprise was waiting. Both men on high alert for an ambush of vicious, shadow creatures. It was then, Sam realized he'd left his knife back at the camp. Now he was the one who was naked. Well, not completely, he did have his little toothbrush-knife in his pocket if he became desperate. It wasn't just the mysterious jungle creatures Sam was worried about. He was also watching Desmond with the same intensity. Afterall, Sam still wasn't sure what happened on the beach that day when he blacked out near the boat.

(The BOAT!)

"Des?

"Yep."

"Where is the boat?"

A good ten-twelve paces went by before Desmond responded. "Boat?"

"The fucking boat, Desmond!" Sam said exasperated. "You know. The one you built a fortress around on the beach. The one you sailed in on like Christ, and then crashed from like Cortez."

Desmond looked at Sam incredulously, if not intolerantly.

"Cortez, eh?...Ah, the boat...Damned if I know. I didn't set her a blaze if that's what you mean."

Sam, even in his anger, was surprised that Desmond caught the reference.

"Where the fuck is it?"

Desmond sincerely looked dumbfounded. "I didn't notice it this morning when I came out here, but I'd bet if she's not there she was lured into the sea by the tide."

He seemed not at all surprised or concerned which just infuriated Sam further. Without thinking, Sam lunged at Desmond and barreled into him like a linebacker in the red zone. Both men tumbled down a slight decline from their path, bouncing off the rocks and tree trunks like pinballs into a shallow puddle of mud and broken limbs. They both lay motionless save for the heaving breaths emanating from their now earth and blood covered faces. Some time passed before they began to stir. They stumbled to get to their feet like professional wrestlers after a double chair shot. Desmond got up first and staggered toward Sam. He swung his bloody mallet of an arm, just barely catching the side of Sam's head. It was enough to send Sam crumbling back to the mud. The momentum of Desmond's flail was enough to send him crumbling down as well.

"What the fuck was that about, mate?" Desmond almost seemed to be laughing through a wheezing, stuttered breath.

"The…(heaving pant) …b-oat…Wh-at did you do to it?"

Desmond lumbered to a seated position against a tree. Sam did as well.

"I don't know where she went, mate. She was gone before I woke up. I checked a bit down the shoreline, but figured the drink got her and broke her down. She's probably at the bottom of the ocean like a blue diamond."

A pain from the fall and the fight started behind Sam's eyes.

"You saw it was gone? Why wouldn't you wake me. This is a pretty big fucking deal, Des!."

"Is it?"

Sam scowled. "It was our-"

"Our what" Desmond interrupted. "It was nothing but a broken-down wreck full of ghosts and heirlooms of a previous life. That's it. No rescue. No escape... No sanity."

Desmond's voice began to trail off a bit.

Sam couldn't find the words to articulate his feelings. He grumbled a bit in both pain and anger. Deep down, he knew Desmond was right and that continuing to argue against it was like arguing against himself. In the distance, a howl swung through the trees like a primal invasion. Sam was so exhausted that it barely piqued his interest.

The noise brought Desmond back from his drift.

"Alright then." He exhaled as he made his way to his feet. He offered a hand to Sam. Sam made his way up alone.

Desmond began to trek back toward their destination. Sam followed a few paces behind, his curiosity getting the better of him. Still, he was guarded. One fist clenched, the other posting up against the trees they passed to help him maintain balance on the uneven terrain.

Desmond began to whistle a song, slow and off-tune. Even though, it had a warm quality to it. Soulful. Melancholy. It lingered gently into Sam's subconscious. Before long he began to picture a scene built around the song. An outdoor cafe? Something of the sort. Cobblestone pavers and wrought iron furniture. The image was misty. Faceless people in the foreground and background alike. He squinted his eyes and leaned into the images in hopes they wouldn't fade. The air smelled like centuries old architecture and warm bread. Well-sipped wine glasses were on the table. Across from him at the table, a woman's figure. Her body language flirty as she laughed and touched his hand. The imaginary gesture made the hairs on Sam's arm stand longingly. The woman's eyes were coming into focus when Sam's attention was startled.

"Just up this ridge, mate." Desmond said patting Sam's shoulder like as reassuring dad.

Sam could only imagine what crazy shit awaited them at the top of the ridge. Desmond lumbered up the last bit ahead of him and then extended an arm. This time, Sam took it and Desmond helped hoist him up with a groan. Sam sprung up swiftly like ricocheting shrapnel. Taking flight from both feet for a second before he landed face to face with a severed head on a wooden stake.

22. Desmond's Past: How Did We Get Here?

Desmond traced his fingers along the dusty outline of the desk where the laptop typically idles. His mind racing. Resting his head in his hands, he tried to rationalize what he saw, but everything he thought he knew to be true came into question. Memories of their relationship began to flood his thoughts. Sea water invading a capsizing ship.

■ ■

Their first date was a few nights after Desmond saved Sheryl from being consumed by the sidewalk outside of the gym on her campus. Desmond, having felt the need to try to impress Sheryl, made them reservations at *the Top* lounge and restaurant. *The Top* was an all glass revolving restaurant at the top of the hotel in town. Desmond had never been there himself. He fancied himself simpler. He thought, however, that a first date at one of his typical go-to's wasn't going to cut it.

That night they had decided to meet at the restaurant. Sheryl had insisted on it as her apartment was nearby. Inside, he felt out of his league, which sat in direct contrast to his outward disposition. He remembered arriving about 15 minutes prior to when they said they'd meet. He wanted a few moments to gather himself and give the appearance that he was waiting for her. But of course, Sheryl was on the bench outside of the hotel when he pulled up. Her smile was more brilliant than the hotel marque. Though his plan to get there first was foiled, he couldn't help but be at ease by Sheryl's glow.

When he approached her, Sheryl greeted him with a warm hug. He could remember her breath hitting his ear. This caused Desmond to breathe deeply. He fixated on that feeling for a moment before allowing his memory to continue.

After their embrace, they headed up to the top floor of the hotel on which the rooftop restaurant was perched. At first, everything felt really casual which put Desmond at ease a bit. He couldn't believe how nervous he was. His palms felt clammy. He rubbed his hands together and smiled as the elevator doors opened. They got in as did a pair of young, yuppie-ish couples. You know. Guys wearing turtlenecks and sportscoats with completely messy, yet somehow perfect looking haircuts. The women in some kind of fancy dresses and pearls. They were giggling way too much and too loudly like they had been pregaming some place prior to their reservations. Their voices echoed off the elevator walls like speakers inside Desmond's head

As the elevator ascended, Sheryl reached out and touched Desmond's hand. He looked curiously. She smiled up at him coyly.

"You're doing great." She whispered with a wink.

"Glad you think so." He whispered back while wiping his brow in jest.

When the elevator let out, they were greeted by magnificence. The lighting in the restaurant was dim, but not annoyingly so. There were two fireplaces across from each other surrounded by oversized leather lounge chairs. There were tables around the perimeter of the room, right up against the floor to ceiling windows which overlooked the city. Prime real estate. Still, there were more tables set up throughout. Elevated slightly as they got further away from the windows. At the center, a huge circular bar with fast moving bartenders. Martini, wine, and highball glasses in the hands of the patrons. Yup…Desmond felt out of place.

The hostess showed Desmond and Sheryl to their table. He had reserved one right up against the window at which Sheryl gave an impressed smile and nod as she sat.

The details of the conversation that he and Sheryl had that night were incredibly hazy in Desmond's mind which is odd considering how many other details he remembered quite vividly. After a short wait the waiter came over and took their drink order, then they began small talk. Desmond's mind was only half-present, feeling distracted by the movement around him. Though he must have been convincing enough in his posture and facial expression to give off the impression that he was attentive and interested (and he *was* interested) because Sheryl didn't seem to notice anything amiss.

Sheryl told him a story during dinner that he can't quite ever remember, but it's one that she has brought up many times in conversation since, and one that he's had to navigate by pretending to know what she was talking about.

The entire restaurant was on a pivot. It rotated clockwise, ever so slowly, so that everyone could see in a three-sixty without having to move around themselves. The movement was almost imperceivable save for the fact that the view changed. It seemed pretty cool at first, but Desmond quickly realized he could perceive the spinning and he definitely did not enjoy it. It all gave him an uneasy feeling that he wasn't in control of his mind. The background view kept changing but the people in the mid ground stayed the same.

Why the fuck did that bother him so much? Desmond just couldn't let it go. His focus should have been on the gorgeous and incredibly interesting woman in front of him, but he just couldn't shake free from the feeling. He felt almost tipsy, and he hadn't even yet taken a sip of his drink.

By the time the entrees came, Desmond shook off his fog. His eyes shifted and Sheryl noticed. Seemingly so much so that she had become aware of the possibility that Desmond hadn't actually been present during much of the night. A curious look fixed itself on her brow for a moment, but she seemed to let it go.

The rest of dinner went better. They shared their favorite dessert, brownie a la mode. They even closed out the night with a sweet peck. On the lips.

■ ■

A few weeks into their relationship, Desmond and Sheryl ended their date at his place. It was the night before Desmond was to take a weekend bachelor party trip for a close friend who, after spending much of his adolescence chasing every girl he laid eyes on, had recently *really committed* to his on again off again college girlfriend. Knowing Desmond would be gone for a few days, both he and Sheryl wanted this night to be special.

Desmond kept a fairly neat home for a bachelor. In fact, Sheryl mentioned she couldn't help but notice that everything seemed to be just so. His apartment opened into a small foyer with a closet. It was well lit. Desmond took Sheryl's coat and put it into the closet.

"This is it." He said modestly.

Sheryl smiled warmly as she made her way toward the living room.

"Can I get you a nightcap?" Desmond asked.

"Sure. She said and followed Desmond to a little bar area at the edge of the room.

"What can I get'cha?" He gestured to an array of bottles on the bar top in his best bartending posture.

"Mmmm, pour me what you're having."

Desmond obliged and grabbed two rocks glasses from the far end of the bar top. He pulled the cork from a bottle of whisky and doled out two healthy pours.

"Ice?"

"Neat." Sheryl said through a bite in her bottom lip.

Desmond carried the two glasses over to the sofa. He handed Sheryl a glass and held his up.

"Here's to the imprint you've already left on my heart." Desmond said in a sincere tone. Then added with a slight smile. "And to the imprint your butt made in the cement where we met."

"Both yours to keep." Sheryl said playfully with a wink.

Desmond raised his eyebrows with a sly smile and a tip of his glass. It was kind of early in the relationship, but they both felt it. There was an undeniable attraction and not just physical. They were in each other's heads in a way neither of them felt before. They both took a long swallow of the whisky. Desmond noticed that Sheryl didn't wince.

The living area in Desmond's apartment wasn't flashy, but it did have a themed feel. Most of the furniture was midcentury modern giving it that 1950's vibe if not for the oversized TV directly across from the sofa.

"Music?" Desmond pointed over to a record player at the edge of the room.

Without a word, Sheryl got up and perused his collection. In it she found what some may see as paradoxes of taste. Sheryl appreciated the eclectic assortment from which to choose. The records were alphabetized and separated by genre. She pulled one from the display, Patsy Cline's "Showcase" album and slid it from the cover. She flipped over the record to side B and laid it onto the player. Looking back a Desmond with a flirty smile she dropped the needle onto the record and after a small pop and sizzle it began to play.

"Crazy. I'm crazy for feeling so lonely…"

Desmond leaned back and put his arm up on the back of the couch.

"Patsy Cline. Good choice."

"Patsy Cline is always a good choice." Sheryl smiled.

Sitting beside him, closely, Sheryl continued to take in the room. It was a modestly sized living space. The leather sofa upon which they sat was a firm statement of a manly feel to the apartment, as was much of the other large furniture, which sat in contrast to some more refined, albeit quirky, pieces around the room giving it a feel as if the apartment were decorated by a team of people with varying tastes. Yet, it all worked somehow. A darkish grey carpet with a seemingly patternless splatter of burgundy designed across the far edge stretched out beneath their feet blanketing a plank wood floor. Scrunching her toes into the tufts of thread, she noticed the rug had a soft, almost massaging sensation against her feet.

A large, heavy, and dark wood bookshelf sat caddy corner. On it were various little knickknacks that you may see in an elderly spinster's place. A miniature wooden mallard sat loudly on the corner of the second shelf from the top. The top shelf was lined with other assorted tiny ceramic animals with these wobbly heads that danced with the vibrations of any movement in the room. On the bottom shelf in the opposite corner of the duck sat a stuffed rabbit with its paws dangling off the edge. It was a little raggedy stuffed rabbit that may have, at one time, been beige, but was now a greyish-brown color almost as if it had been singed. An aged and worn-out child's toy from the past perhaps. She bent down to take a closer look at it. It looked as if it had been resewn a few times. Various colored stitching with loose ends here and there. Sheryl reached out to touch it, but as she did, she felt Desmond's position on the couch shift. She paused her reach and then stood back up at the shelf.

"It's from when I was a kid." Desmond started. "The rabbit is."

"Oh?" Sheryl replied

"Yea, kinda like my imaginary friend growing up. You know. A best mate. But don't worry." He said in jest. "We haven't spoken in a while."

As curious as it was, Sheryl nodded with a raised brow and let it be. She turned her focus toward the books. They were arranged in a variety of ways. Some standing upright. Others in stacks on their backs. Much unlike the records, the books weren't separated by genre. Just simply arranged in a way that gave them a curated appearance. Sheryl could tell though that they weren't there merely for display. Many of them looked well used which made her smile to herself as she was a veracious reader herself.

Desmond watched intently as Sheryl made herself at home. She touched her fingertips to a few titles on the bookshelf and then turned.

"Quite the collection." She gestured.

"Yeah, I um. Had some of that stuff since I was a kid. And some of them, I don't really remember where I got them." Desmond stammered.

Sheryl noticed this and eased the pressure a bit.

"The books." She assured him. "I love books! Some of my favorite nights have been spent alone immersed in a story."

"Oh, the books. Yea. Me too. I like the feeling of living in someone else's mind. Being in whole other lives just from words on a page."

Sheryl sat back onto the sofa, close to Desmond.

"Do you have any favorites?" she asked.

Desmond sighed thoughtfully. "That's tough. I'm kinda all over the place."

"I can see that." Sheryl teased pointing toward the shelves.

"What are you reading now?"

"Right now." Desmond started. "I'm reading these." Desmond pulled two books from the side table near where he was seated and handed them to Sheryl.

"In the Heart of the Sea." She read aloud. "…and", she continued with an incredulous look. "Based on a True Story".

"You're reading both of these together?"

"Yea, well, not together." Desmond started. "Heart of the Sea is a pretty heavy book. Whenever I read something with weight to it, I like to have something light close by to wind my gears back down."

"What about you? Reading anything?"

Sheryl smiled as she read the back covers of the books Desmond gave her.

"I like to read a few at a time too." She smiled. "But usually, I read a new book and have one handy that I've previously read. I enjoy revisiting novels. Right now, I am reading a novel by one of my favorite authors called 3rd Degree. It's a thrilling novel so far."

"And on reserve?" Desmond smiled

"Jane Eyre. I'm a sucker for the classics."

"Maybe we'll read some books together so we can talk about them. Start a book club so we can get inside other minds together." Desmond mused.

"I'd like that." Sheryl agreed.

Desmond saw the perfect opportunity for a kiss, but Sheryl beat him to it. She moved swiftly and placed her lips on his. Eventually, they made it from the sofa to the bedroom.

The next morning, Sheryl woke to Desmond gathering his clothes into a travel bag for his trip. She stretched out with a contented sigh. As she did the sheet fell from her neck revealing her naked torso.

"Good morning." She smiled.

Desmond's head popped up from his bag to the pleasantries.

"Hey." He smiled. "How'd you sleep?"

Sheryl began to get herself together. "Pretty well. Some night."

"It was…pretty damn amazing. Sorry I gotta leave this morning. I wish I didn't."

"Me too." Sheryl said. "Do you have time to get some breakfast?"

"Definitely. And no worries. I'll be back in a few days, and we'll start our book club." Desmond winked.

"It's a date." Sheryl replied.

"Oh, and here." Desmond reached his hand out to her. In it were a few papers.

Sheryl took them. "What's this?"

"It's the last few pages from the book I'm reading. I want you to hold onto them for safe keeping. This way you know I have to come back to you. If I ever want to know how the story ends that is." Desmond smiled playfully.

"You are a smoothie." Sheryl jested. And off they went.

■ ■

The relationship was budding nicely. The street they walked was lined with daffodils.

"These are my favorite." Sheryl said as she leaned into Desmond's arm.

Desmond's eyes puzzled.

"Daffodils", she continued. "They're really quite special."

"They are something, but I always thought they looked depressed." Desmond offered.

"That's just it." Sheryl breathed. "Their beauty is a tragic reflection of the fragility of life. Of love."

"Oh?" Desmond wondered aloud.

She smiled at the invitation to expound and paused their step.

She knelt and placed the ridge of her forefinger under one of the flower bulbs gently raising it upward like a reassuring mom would an upset child.

"You see how the bulbs seem to be gazing downward? It's said that they formed that way as a reflection of the Greek hunter, Narcissus.

"The god?" Desmond interjected.

"Well, he was born from gods, but Narcissus was actually mortal." She continued. "His arrogance caused him to fixate on his own reflection in a pool of water where he was transformed into the flower. So, they say, the flower took on his posture, gazing into his own eyes."

"So, your favorite flower has a vanity problem, eh?" Desmond jested as he mockingly adjusted his hair.

"When I look at them, I don't see that at all." Sheryl said through a smile.

"Look closely. Can you see. There is a sad, shameful expression permeating from the petals. An almost melancholy plead. Like, if you asked them what's wrong, they'd throw their leaves around you in an embrace and begin weeping…"

Sheryl squeezed Desmond's arm and rose to embrace him. With her face close to his, she continued.

"It's as if they are paying for the sins of Narcissus. They spend their life sharing their beauty yet are destined to never face the sun."

Sheryl's mind fascinated Desmond. He would gladly pay for an all-day ticket to ride along the tracks of her thoughts, exploring how they all connected.

"Here", she said. "Smell this one."

"Eww!" Desmond gasped as he withdrew from the flower's bulb. "That smells something terrible."

"It does." She replied

"Shame something so beautiful can be so repulsive." Desmond said smartly.

Sheryl smiled even more and took a slow soothing whiff near a different bulb.

"Now this one."

"No chance…Fool me once…" Desmond said trailing.

"No, really. Smell."

Desmond acquiesced and breathed deeply the sweet flower.

"Wow. That smells…" he didn't have the words.

"Lovely!" Sheryl finished.

"Right. Why so different?" Desmond wondered knowing that Sheryl had more within her to share.

"Love." She replied. "The first flower we smelled isn't getting what it needs most. Its odor reflects the lack of care and attention it's received. The flower, like us, needs to be loved. Without love, it becomes depressed and turns foul. The second flower, the one that smelled sweet, is giving back to the world the beauty it has felt."

"So, this is like a metaphor then?" Desmond said ironically.

"Maybe." Sheryl smiled.

"I better treat you right then. Don't want you stinking up the joint." Desmond mocked lightheartedly.

Luckily the joke was received playfully, and Sheryl squeezed his arm more tightly and nuzzled against him.

"You're darn tootin'," Sheryl giggled."

■ ■

The memory made Desmond pause his thoughts. Eyes closed, he could smell the sweet daffodil with such intensity, he raised his face toward the sun in a revolt against any shame. With his next breath the putrid stench of his sins wafted into his mind like the penetrating odor from the other daffodil had all those years ago and he found himself gagging into another bed of memories.

■ ■

He hadn't meant to put his hands on Sheryl. He never hit her. Never! That's what he repeated to himself over and over after he apparently lost control all those years ago. He didn't even truly remember what he did. His memory of it, instead, was patched together from Sheryl's recollections which she subsequently shared with their therapist. It was only once, but once was enough to sour a part of their intimacy seemingly forever.

Desmond and Sheryl had decided to move in together. This was a big step for Sheryl. The first time she would be sharing a home with anyone besides her beagle, Pepper. This would be the first time Desmond would be living with a girlfriend as well, however he had, on occasion, been in relationships where a woman he'd been seeing would stay at his apartment for extended periods. Desmond never had a pet before. As a boy, he wasn't allowed to have one and then as time and absence would have it, he never grew too fond of the idea. Plus, he didn't have allergies per se, but he noted an uptick in sneezing whenever he would be around pets for too long. Nonetheless, Sheryl and Pepper were a package deal so whatever reservations or reactions Desmond had about dogs, he would have to suppress or get over them.

Sheryl got Pepper as a pup and had her for a few years prior to she and Desmond meeting. They were protective of each other. Desmond didn't mind Pepper all that much generally, though it was clear that she did not like it when Desmond and Sheryl got too close. She wouldn't bite or growl really, but she'd bark and bounce in attempts to disrupt them. One could see how this could become at least mildly irritating. Whatever small irritations Pepper gave Desmond, they weren't overwhelming enough to deter him from Sheryl.

They were still in what Desmond would consider to be the honeymoon phase of their relationship and Desmond had a plan to propose to Sheryl on their first night in their new home together. He had the ring for a while. Actually, he had two rings. One he picked up at a small jewelry shop. The shop, in fact, was on the same block where they discovered the trove of daffodils a while back. Like the sweet-smelling flowers, the ring was beautiful. The diamond at the center was modest, but shined brightly, reflecting the light like a prism. Around it was a ring of small stones of various shades and colors. A perfect combination of refined beauty and playfulness, Desmond thought. An inscription within the band read, "M.A.D."

The second ring was one which he had since he was young. It originally belonged to his mother and was one of the few things that remained after the fire. It too was modest. It had just one diamond in the center with no other stones. Beautiful no doubt, however, Desmond wasn't really sure why he still had it. It was somewhat tarnished and, compared to the ring he'd purchased, was of lesser quality.

The ring was just about the only tangible thing he possessed that connected him directly to his mother. Consequently, there was baggage attached to it that, whenever he looked at the ring, caused him to feel any number of things from nostalgia to remorse to contempt. Emotions that flooded his brain and waged war against each other for possession of his psyche. The fate of each seemingly decided by moral luck whenever they clashed.

It's not that Maggie was a bad mother. Quite the contrary in some regards. She loved Desmond the best way she knew how. Yet she was feckless, even indifferent, to the circumstances that loomed over his childhood and their family. Nonetheless, Desmond loved his mother, and he couldn't simply get rid of the ring. Nothing about his relationship with his family's past was quite that simple.

Desmond was left with a decision that appeared to be an easy one. The ring he bought for Sheryl had a pure sentimental quality. He bought it, after all, where one of their most amazing nights took place. It was perfect for her and the best way to showcase his love. If all went well, and Desmond got the nerve, he'd use it to propose. He could always give Sheryl his mother's ring later, after they were married. For an anniversary perhaps. By then, he imagined, any negative effects the ring may have had on his mentality will have eroded.

Both Sheryl and Desmond had a full life's worth of stuff. They decided a mix-and-max approach to their furniture would be best. Regarding their personal effects, the smaller items and display pieces, they made a deal with each other that some couples might find stressful and invasive, but they both rather enjoyed. They allowed for two standard sized medium packing boxes each. Whatever they could fit inside them, they agreed to find a spot for inside their newly shared space. This challenge, of course, didn't pertain to either of their respective book collections. They both had pretty substantial libraries and they both saw their collections of literature as non-negotiables. For these items Desmond and Sheryl had to buy quite a few shipping boxes.

The movers had come and delivered everything early in the morning. Sheryl had coffee brewing even earlier in a pot which she and Desmond picked out together. She knew that copious amounts of caffeine would be in order if they were to take on the task of setting up their new home together.

"To us and ours." Sheryl offered raising her coffee mug to celebrate with a toast and a wink.

"Here, here." Desmond added with a wink of his own and clanked his mug to hers in an overacted manner.

A few errands pushed their unpacking into the afternoon. That was fine by Desmond as he wanted to propose after their first dinner together at home. They'd order take-out as neither of them would feel like cooking after a long day. He had, in the fridge, a package of mini cakes from a bakery that Sheryl adored hidden behind various everyday refrigerated stuff. A bottle of wine they were saving for an occasion such as this was on reserve in one of the boxes. He figured that after they ate, they can relax a bit in the living room and listen to some music. Then, he'd present her with dessert and the ring. A perfect beginning at the end of a perfect night.

After they arrived back home, it didn't take very long to get the furniture situated since they had the movers bring the larger items directly to the rooms in which they would rest. Sheryl had already started laundry so that they would have fresh sheets for their bed. Most of the rest of the afternoon was spent organizing their books. They decided to organize them loosely by genre, but also alternating stacks and columns like Desmond had at his previous apartment. Pepper spent the afternoon exploring the space, sniffing out each nook and cranny until finally curling up on the floor in the warmth of the sliding glass door off the kitchen.

When the take-out arrived, there were just a few boxes left to sort through. They ordered from an Italian restaurant that seemed to have good reviews. Desmond shuffled through his boxes to retrieve the wine while Sheryl set the food onto the plates. Desmond found the box containing the wine and with a key from his keyring sliced open the packing tape. He opened the box. In it was the wine, the stuffed rabbit, the mallard, and a few other trinkets he kept for display. He pulled the wine from the box, unwrapped it from the bubble wrap, and strolled back toward Sheryl who was already waiting at the table.

"Thought we'd open this to celebrate." Desmond displayed the bottle.

"Ah, nice." Sheryl exclaimed. "If there ever were an occasion." She trailed.

Desmond opened the wine, poured two healthy glasses, and once again they toasted. Everything was perfect.

They were midway through dinner when Pepper began to wander about beneath the table. Normally, it somewhat annoyed Desmond when Pepper would brush up against his legs during dinner, but either he was no longer bothered by it, or the wine loosened him up. Either way it was notable in his mind. He even looked down and went to pet her.

"Hey. Pepper has something in her mouth."

"Oh no, can you get it?" Sheryl replied

At first, Desmond didn't think much of it. He reached down to grab Pepper's collar and tug whatever it was from her jaw. As he reached down though, Pepper ran to the far end of the table. Sheryl stood up as did Desmond.

"Come here girl." Sheryl coaxed, but Pepper was reluctant, moving about in a hopping side to side motion looking for an escape.

"Come on, Pep!" Sheryl tried again. "She thinks we're playing."

Desmond took a swill of his wine and placed the glass down to get ready to catch the dog. Sheryl could see the seriousness in Desmond's eyes and when he looked over at her she giggled at him. Surprised, Desmond giggled as well despite himself, momentarily lightening the moment. He stepped toward her, and Pepper bolted under the table into the kitchen. As she did, her body hit one of the chairs consequently shaking the table and nearly knocking over Desmond's wine glass. Both Desmond and Sheryl gave playful chase into the next room. What could have felt like calamity instead was turning into a sillyl memory for them to share of their first night in their new home.

They finally captured Pepper in the living room. A joint effort. When they were able to wrestle the object from her mouth, Desmond recognized it instantly. His smile evaporated quicker than water in a desert mirage. He held up the object and like a switch he was almost unrecognizable.

"What is it?" Sheryl puzzled.

"Son of a bitch." Desmond whisper yelled through clenched teeth.

Sheryl's face wrinkled up in concern. "What? What's the matter, Des?"

Desmond stood up without a word and walked quickly over to the moving boxes. Sheryl remained on the floor with the dog, holding her as if bracing against something awful.

"Son of a bitch, bitch." Desmond called out.

He reached down behind the box that he had previously opened for the wine and pulled up from the floor a bundle of raggedy tufts of cotton and fabric. At first Sheryl had no idea what it was. Then she noticed the long strand of thread hanging down from Desmond's clenched hand. At the thread's end, a big brown button. It was Desmond's rabbit.

"Oh God." Sheryl exclaimed knowing that the rabbit was important to Desmond. Perhaps, not truly understanding how important.

"I'm sorry, Des." She sincerely pled.

"Fuckin' mutt." Desmond accused.

"Desmond?" Sheryl broke in. "Pep didn't mean it. She's just a dog. I know that rabbit meant-"

"What do you know?" Desmond cut her off.

"Desmond." Sheryl's tone got tense. "It was an accident. It wasn't her fault."

"Wasn't her fault?" Desmond shot back incredulously.

It's as if he blacked out. He took two quick strides toward Sheryl and Pepper and reached down to grab Pepper's collar. As he grabbed it, Sheryl shot up and began to shove Desmond.

"What are you doing?" She cried, flailing to keep him away.

Desmond's anger bubbled over, radiating through his skin. Sheryl pushed him again, but this time when she did, Desmond grabbed her hard by the arms and his body tensed into a clench. Pepper was barking erratically and jumping up at Desmond's side. Sheryl tried to break free, but Desmond's grip engulfed her. Their eyes met and, for a moment, Sheryl could see her own frightened expression in them. Tears were running down her cheek. The ordeal felt slow motion and sped up all at once like the microsecond before an atom bomb explodes. Then, as suddenly as a power outage, Desmond's hands let go. His arms fell limply to his side and his head fell to his chest. He let out a long heavy exhale knowing that the fallout would be severe. Sheryl bent down crying, clutching Pepper in her arms. Desmond put his hands over his face in shame.

"Sheryl." He whimpered. "I - I'm sorry."

He fell to Sheryl's side. Tears now running down his cheeks as well. He meekly reached out to touch Sheryl's shoulder. She recoiled in protest. It was a long time, maybe hours, before either of them moved or spoke.

When they finally did, Sheryl was the first to move. She stood without a word and began to clean up the remnants of a dinner that felt like a world away. After a few minutes, Desmond followed. He begged silently with an impotent posture. Sheryl relented and let Desmond talk to her.

He had a million things he wanted to say. To try to provide rationale behind losing his temper, but there was no excuse for his actions. Deep down, even he knew that. He instead said just that.

"There is no excuse for what I just did." He began. "There are a million things I want to tell you, but I know that nothing I can say would absolve me from my actions tonight…"

Sheryl stopped cleaning up and stared Desmond in the eye as he spoke. Lips held tight. The tension in her jaw was visible through her skin.

"I am truly sorry, Sheryl. No one, let alone you, deserves to be treated that way. If you want me to leave, just say and I'll go."

Desmond stood there for a moment hoping for any kind of response. Even if Sheryl were to tell him to get the fuck out. Anything. But Sheryl didn't say a word. She just walked past him to the bedroom and closed the door. Desmond sat down at the dining room table and poured a glass of wine. He held up the glass to the air and then tipped it to his lips.

After an hour or so, Desmond heard the bedroom door open. He looked up and saw an empty hallway, the door left open. Sheryl's silent invitation into the bedroom. Desmond sighed a sigh of relief. He stood up and straightened himself out. Mindlessly, he put his hand in the pocket of his pants. From it he pulled out his mother's ring, the ring he'd purchased, and the stuffed rabbit's foot which he pulled from Pepper's mouth earlier. He gently jiggled them in his hand. He held up the two rings. He placed the ring he bought back into his pocket and tossed his mother's ring into the trash. He held the rabbit's foot tightly in his hand. Then, he took a deep breath and headed toward the bedroom.

.. ■

Desmond jolted out of that memory without playing the rest out in his mind. He felt disgusted with himself and also, somehow disgusted with Sheryl. One way or another, he was able to convince Sheryl that he would prove himself to her, vowing to never put her through anything like that again. At the time, Desmond recalled, he felt like he was given an opportunity he didn't deserve. Now, he wasn't so sure. Now, everything felt like a curse. He began to drift back into his memories hoping to land in one to bring him out of this black hole. Instead, it only got darker.

.. ■

It was Christmas season. Desmond and Sheryl had been married for a few years and they were getting ready to go to her staff party. She was in the bathroom *putting on her face.* He found himself standing in front of the bedroom mirror. The knot in his tie was not cooperating. He pulled at it vehemently like he was escaping from a noose that somehow malfunctioned. Ripping it from his neck he threw it angrily on the floor and unbuttoned the top button of his dress shirt to gasp a breath of freedom. Staring down at the tie, he grumbled incoherently in a way that, if the tie were alive, it would have taken it as a declaration of war. But it wasn't the tie Desmond was upset at. He had been upset often those days. Nothing seemed to be going his way and this party, this party, was a big old jolly slap in his face.

A pain rose in Desmond's head at the bridge of his nose. He pinched it and sat on the bed's edge. About two and a half months prior, Desmond lost his job. Since then, he grew more and more bitter. Sheryl did her best not to pressure him about the bills, but it was nearing the three-month mark and Desmond seemed to be slipping further and further from any prospects.

Honestly, he was lucky that all his boss did was fire him and that he wasn't brought up on charges. It was early October and Desmond was on a job site to build some new apartments overlooking the river. Sheryl surprised Desmond with some lunch from his favorite deli. She knew better than to try to wander around an active construction site, so she went straight toward the trailer in which the site boss usually sat monitoring the walkies and directing the project.

Sheryl walked cautiously up the thin metal steps to the trailer door and gave it a knock. The door pushed open to reveal Desmond's boss yelling on the phone to some apparent "jerk-off" about a delayed delivery. His eyes caught her, and he waved her in. Sheryl stepped across the threshold of the trailer and waited near, not on, a small sofa of a makeshift meeting area within. Desmond's boss finished his phone call and brought his attention up to her after tossing a pencil to the desk with a reserved frustration.

"Hey Sheryl." Carl said through a sigh that was left over from his previous exchange.

"Here to see Desmond?"

"No, actually. I brought this sandwich for you." Sheryl said in a lighthearted, yet sarcastic way.

Sheryl had stopped by the various jobsites from time to time to bring Desmond his lunch and over the years, outside of work, Carl and Desmond have gone out for the occasionally drink. They were much less a boss and employee, but more like buddies. Sheryl and Desmond had even had Carl and his wife to the house a few times for dinner.

"I'll call him down." Carl told her through an easy smile.

Sheryl had that effect on people around her. Something natural to her personality that made people feel comfortable and less stressed.

"Thanks." She smiled back. Sheryl took a seat on the couch. Carl called Desmond down on the walkie. and then went on to look over some plans.

Sheryl glanced around on the coffee table at a few scattered magazines. Mostly they were about landscaping and construction stuff with a few *nudie* mags sprinkled in. She found herself quickly bored of that and made her way toward Carl.

"Whatcha working on?" She asked sincerely.

"We're bidding on a new project for the city. That's who I was on the phone with. One of the guys at the city planning office. He's a real piece of work."

"Can I see the plans?" Without waiting for a response, Sheryl came closer to Carl having a genuine interest in seeing the building prints.

Her personality lent itself to Sheryl seeming overly friendly in a world of standoffish people. To some, she had a flirtatious manner, but really, she just enjoyed people. There wasn't anything flirtatious or inappropriate in Sheryl's body language, though she always wore outfits that flattered her body, and it was hard not to notice. Carl wasn't blind. He caught himself glancing, but he wasn't the type to make advances toward another woman. Currently, Sheryl was wearing a fitted floral top that looked similar to a summer dress and form fitting high waist jeans, cuffed at the bottom exposing her ankles. She rounded off the outfit with some all-white sneakers. It was just a normal outfit, but she wore it well.

Carl began pointing out a few of the buildings potential features and while they chatted it up, their respective proximity to each other mindlessly fluctuated. As they continued, Sheryl did notice Carl as well. Standing over six feet tall, even taller than Desmond, Carl was a solid man built from years of laboring. No crime in silent admiration. Perhaps it was their familiarity or the ease in which they talked that caused their sway. Innocently, their arms brushed each other. It was just then, Desmond walked in. If not for the quick jump of panic and flustered manner in which Sheryl began speaking, Desmond might not have felt as though anything was off, but it was enough to trigger something within him. Without a word or hesitation, Desmond snatched up Carl by the shirt with one hand and pummeled him in the eye with the other. The men rolled about the office with such ferocity, plans flew about and fell to the ground like a snowstorm. When it was all said and done, Desmond ended up fired, Sheryl and Desmond ended up in counseling, and Carl spent a week on liquid lunches.

Sheryl and Desmond began their sessions almost immediately after this incident, though they had talked more than once about their need for counseling for quite some time. Sheryl, in Desmond's estimation, was no longer attracted to him. He confided in the doctor as much in their first session. Desmond, Sheryl expressed, had become paranoid and easily irritated. Both Sheryl and Desmond knew that they loved each other and wanted to figure this thing out.

In the few sessions between the principal one and the night of Christmas party, Desmond further laid out the evidence of Sheryl's diminished desire toward him. It hadn't been that long since they had been intimate, but it was edging on a year since that intimacy was a result of his advancements rather than at her occasional whim and no time else. He felt increasingly unwanted and impotent. His logical conclusion was that Sheryl no longer loved him. At least not in the way that lovers love.

Was Desmond reading too much into it? Life in marriage is long. It is full of lulls. Passion and connection ebb and flow. Whispering tides on island shores. Notwithstanding the gaps in intimacy, Sheryl was the perfect wife. She always took care of Desmond and the home they built together. Perhaps, that was part of the problem.

Sheryl naturally felt attacked by Desmond's contentions. What about his role in all of this? What had he done to warrant the uncontrollable desire and need for intimacy he expected to illicit from her? Was the burden of keeping the fire kindled solely on her?

Sheryl did her best to unpack the heavy bags of their issues trying to itemize the how and why they got to the point they were in their relationship. She was willing to accept some of the responsibility for their intimacy issues. She, at times, would get stuck on things that bothered her and, admittedly, it took her a long time to work through them regardless of how insignificant they may seem to him. She recognized as much, but she wasn't going to shoulder the blame all on her own. In fact, she pointed out, much of this tension resulted from what she called Desmond's *shifts*. Like the incident with her dog, Pepper, who subsequently passed away later that year. Desmond's shifts, which Sheryl told the therapist Desmond attributed to "*messed up childhood*", were not frequent, but when they occurred caused dramatic changes to their relationship. Desmond would often use that phrase about his childhood when he couldn't process his emotions or when he reacted in a way that wasn't normal. An avenue down which the therapist would be sure to travel during a future session.

Sheryl had fallen in love with a self-assured man who had a quick wit and strong knowhow, but in the past year or so, he'd been acting like a neutered dog. She didn't use those words. Sheryl would never intentionally hurt Desmond like that, but those words did dance on the tip of her tongue while she reworked the thought into a more palatable phrase. On top of that, Desmond had also become needlessly jealous. Though none of his previous outbursts were comparable with the one that sent Carl to the hospital, he had aggressively accused Sheryl of flirting, even cheating, in the past.

Both Sheryl and Desmond believed they wanted to revive their relationship. They put in a real effort in the meetings and at home to right the ship before it became completely wrecked on the shores of love lost.

(You are the sun shining down on my world. I am but a shameful daffodil struggling to feel the warmth of your love melt away the putrid stench of my sins.)

Sheryl came into the room to find Desmond sitting impotently on the edge of the bed. He was still lost somewhere in the memory of the happenings over the past few months.

"Desmond?" she prodded with a peck. "Here, let me help you with that."

He came to. "Thanks, Darlin'."

"You were in your head pretty deep. You ok?" Sheryl wondered as she knotted a half-Windsor.

"Yea." Desmond replied on a deep but quiet inhale. "Just getting my head right for the evening is all."

"Did you take your pill?" rattling a prescription bottle.

"Just about to." Desmond assured her. "Can you hand me one?"

Sheryl obliged with a reassuring squeeze of the shoulder as Desmond hard swallowed. They stood together in the tall mirror on the wall opposite the edge of their bed and smiled lightly at each other's reflection before heading out for the night.

Though Desmond didn't actually remember the events of the party well, he had to make amends for what transpired for quite some time after. He apparently had some kind of delusionary side effect from mixing his prescription with a few drinks and in the middle of one of those ridiculous line dances like the *Cha-Cha Slide,* he caused a scene on the dance floor during which he called Sheryl a *cheating, lying incarnation of Aphrodite*. Though the outburst was only heard by a few of Sheryl's coworkers, it was enough to render her completely embarrassed and earn him a guest spot at her campus's watercooler for a while.

It took a long time and a *lot* of work for Desmond to earn his way back into the warmth of Sheryl's light, yet he did. Didn't he? Or do inflictions against the heart never truly heal, but instead ooze, perpetually infecting a person with resentment?

■ ■

Desmond cringed away from that memory back to the office desk at which he sat. He felt trapped in the reflection of his sins. He couldn't imagine life without Sheryl in it. Nor could he come to grips with the idea that she would commit the ultimate sin against their marriage.

(Maybe it was nothing and I'm just being paranoid...)

(COME ON, MAN! She'S OBViOUsLY FUCKinG sOMEONE.)

(The email could have been about anything…)

(WaKE UP!)

(That bitch!)

(nOW YOU'RE FUCKING GeTTING IT!)

It was no use. Desmond couldn't shake it. Sheryl had been warming up someone else's flower bed. No fucking way Desmond was going to let that be his curse.

23. The Island: Sacrifice

Congealed blood fell from the ragged ends of the severed head in small chunks, exploding to the ground like missiles in a silent movie. Sam was a statue, cemented in fear. Desmond stood behind the monkey's head holding it from the top like Perseus after destroying an enemy. It took a moment for Sam to regain his faculties.

"What the actual fuck!" he exclaimed.

"Isn't she a beaut?" Desmond touted like an old fisherman.

Sam stammered in his words. "Wh-what did you do?"

"Me? Do?" Desmond said curiously. "He was like this when I found him. I came across this trophy when I was out here…exploring. Place was set up like a primitive sacrifice to the monkey gods."

"You didn't do this?" Sam asked erratically. "Then who did?"

Desmond tilted his head with a knowing smile.

"I didn't fucking do this, Desmond."

"Well then, I guess we aren't alone on this rock after all, eh?" Desmond said with a chummy prod.

(Yeah, maybe it was that other guy you were talking to when you crashed here, Des. Don't think I forgot about that shit.)

Howls swept across the trees sending chills down Sam's arms.

Desmond raised an eyebrow to the sound of the howler monkeys in the trees around them.

"I guess we know who the monsters in the woods are, then."

(Not remotely)

24. The Island: Bird's Eye View

Sam scanned his periphery. The view from this ridge was actually quite spectacular minus the horrifically bloody monkey shrine and the half-cocked nut bag beside him. Walking around the stake he climbed up onto a large boulder that stood away from the edge. From the top, he could see the entire stretch of the island in all directions. Surrounding it, a sea of blackness with no end in sight. Sam scanned the treetops and could see movement within them giving the impression of wildlife going about its business.

Looking downward, Sam noticed this perch offered a good vantage point to observe the island floor as well. He could see discernable objects and matted down pathways for a varied distance around the base. Creeping vines and thick areas in one direction. More clearings in the opposite direction. He felt like a whaler in a crow's nest atop a ship to nowhere. Directionless, Sam was about to step down when from the corner of his eye he saw something out of place. He squinted in concentration and realized what he was seeing. Down the ridge, about thirty to fifty yards out, there was a bit of a clearing near some fallen trees. Marooned beside them was Desmond's rescue boat.

Despite his shock, Sam was able to maintain some assemblance of nonchalance. Just enough so, that Desmond didn't seem to catch anything regarding his demeanor a miss. Sam made a mental note of the general direction of the boat and proceeded to climb down from the rock. Desmond was waiting on the ridge closely.

Sam pushed the base of his palms into the spots directly near the corners of his eyes and pushed inward moving them in an exasperated rotation. Then ran them down his face and over his lips drawing them down in to clenched fists.

25. Shipwrecked: Chum

The splash came from the trail end of Desmond's line, though nowhere close to his makeshift hook. He sprang up into a ready stance sending the boat into a steady rock. The men waited ears wide open for another sign of life. A gurgle emanated from their right and they spun around to see it. A white whale!

No, a small turtle, but destruction lay in its wake, nonetheless.

"Ishmael!" Desmond pointed in an overly dramatic fashion. "Grab the net!"

"Here!" The net floated through the air from the other end of their *Pequod* into Desmond's hands. The sun was glistening off the sweat on his brow and some dripped into his right eye causing him to squint. He stuck out his tongue for balance and held out his thumb for aiming distance. Then, he let the net fly. The moment felt silent as they watched the net soar.

"Direct hit!" Desmond exclaimed. The net landed directly over the turtle, and it swiftly managed to get its head caught between the weaves.

Desmond began to pull the net, but, as he did, the turtle began to wiggle free. Frantically, he yelled out.

"Jump! Get in after her and grab that beautiful beast!"

Without a word or hesitation, his mate plunged into the water after their would-be feast. Swimming along side the line he reached out to grab the net and resecure the turtle. With his hand just about to grab the turtles throat, he felt the hairs on the back of his neck stand up. In the same instant a shadow expanded beneath him from the distance like a black hole. The shadow swallowed the sea beneath him and with it, his ability to breathe.

For the first time, maybe in his life, Desmond was speechless. His mate, jolted on adrenaline at the last second away from the emerging monster. He moved just too late. A goliath grouper broke the surface of the water and swallowed the turtle and the net whole. In the process, the grouper's teeth ripped across his midsection. He was now literal chum. Irony and blood filled the water around him.

26. Desmond's Past: Private Eyes

It had been almost a week of following around Sheryl. So far, aside from some undisclosed shopping at a department store, she hadn't gone anywhere or done anything suspect. Her daily routine was just that. Routine. Even during the most mundane space and time, Sheryl occupied that space in a way that commanded attention. It's not that she sought attention or anything. Nonetheless, her presence in a room was noticed.

Desmond caught himself on multiple occasions inside of daydreams when he was supposed to be on the job proving Sheryl's infidelity. He was waiting at the far end of the parking lot adjacent from the building in which her classroom was. He'd even gone as far as to rent a car to go unnoticed by her as he played private eye. It was a tricky endeavor following a person.

First of all, you had to follow them around without being noticed. In the movies, a tail is almost always spotted. So, Desmond used what he learned during years of research watching crime movies and made sure he kept at least two car lengths distance and stayed in an adjacent lane. On top of that was the waiting around. How do you occupy your time when you are waiting to catch your wife fucking around on you? The radio offers no help. One on a stakeout hardly feels like humming along to whatever 5 songs the station has on repeat at the moment. Napping is out. Its difficult to look inconspicuous when you are sitting in a car for hours. To that end, Desmond decided, he'd have to move the car in and out of the parking lot from time to time to give the illusion that he had a good reason to be on campus.

He could get out of the car and walk around a bit. The campus had a nice long path for joggers and bikes. The risk there is bumping into someone who might recognize him. Even if the odds were slight, it was best to just remain in the car and hope that he blended in enough to not raise the suspicion of security or some student playing campus monitor. No, walking around was out of the question for now.

He sighed deeply and ran his hand down his face. His head involuntarily shook slightly as he played his life out on a loop in his mind.

(Why are we here?)

Some classes had just been let out and the campus was full of noise. Easy enough to go unnoticed as those passing by were mostly engrossed in whatever nonsensical chatter in which young eighteen to twenty-year-olds engage. As Desmond people watched, he started to wonder who Sheryl might be cheating on him with. Her department head? An adjunct? That dickhead colleague of hers with whom he saw her talking at that Christmas party all that time ago? A student?

Desmond flinched. His thoughts had him mindlessly biting his thumbnail. He bit the outer edge too close and tore the skin a bit. When his eyes refocused, he looked up out of the windshield just as a group of young sorority sisters passed by. Two of them looked over as they passed and one of them said something to the other. They giggled, covering their mouths as they continued. This pissed Desmond off more than it probably should have. Somehow, it made him feel helpless. Like an old dog whose owner left him inside of a hot car with the windows up, gasping his final breaths, while she goes into the pet store to find a replacement emotional support animal. He cracked his knuckles. Hard.

Setting his focus on a knoll on the opposite edge of the parking lot, Desmond noticed a groundhog messing around behind some clumps of newly cut grass. It must have been quite some time since the groundskeeper trimmed it as the clippings were abundant. He fixated on the ground hog as it moved. It came out from behind the clippings. Not a groundhog. It was a rabbit. It hopped diagonally down and across the knoll until it was almost directly across from the Desmond's rental. Then, it stopped. Desmond would have sworn it was looking at him. A garbage truck shook them both from the moment. Desmond shivered. The rabbit hopped off, back to the other side of the knoll.

Eventually, Sheryl came out of her building and walked to her car. Desmond supposed this was fairly common since he knew she had a break in her scheduled classes. She started the car and began to pull out of the lot. Desmond followed observing the *rules* of tailing. Sheryl continued off campus and onto the main road. It wasn't a highway, but in each direction, there were 2 lanes for traffic and traffic lights every few blocks.

Even in his self-righteousness, Desmond also felt a bit nervous and unjustified. The contradiction played in his mind like and angel and devil on his shoulders.

"Shit"! Desmond exclaimed

Sheryl had made it through a light as it was turning red. Desmond sped up to try to catch it as well but was trapped behind a guy with some heavily faded political bumper stickers. He attempted to swerve into the connecting turn lane but was boxed in on his left by some *douche* in a BMW. His knuckles were white with frustration and panic. His head was wrenched forward and to the side trying to maintain eye contact with Sheryl's car. Luckily, he saw Sheryl pull into the lot of an upcoming strip mall. The traffic light took agonizingly long to change like the school clock at 2:59pm on the last day before summer break. Finally, it turned, and Desmond sped forward to make up some ground. He pulled into the parking lot and drove around. He couldn't find her car anywhere.

"Where the fuck are you?" He muttered.

Desmond knew he couldn't just drive around the lot endlessly. That would be too exposing. So, he drove to the area of the lot where the diner was and pulled into a spot next to one of those little white box trucks used by electricians and gutter guys. From this spot, hiis periphery was obscured on either side and he couldn't clearly see the doors of the diner. He could see into the windows though. Which, he thought, means that the diner's occupants could see him. He looked around the rental car aimlessly for something…a hat? He didn't know.

Nonetheless, there was nothing to cover his head and, even if there were, it might have just made him look more conspicuous.

A few minutes passed and the truck in the neighboring spot began to pull out.

"Finally." He thought out loud in a huff. "Now I can get a better view of everything."

The truck pulled back to reveal another car in the space two over. In the car's driver seat was Sheryl.

"Shit!" Desmond whisper screamed.

He quickly reached down to the side of his seat and pulled the back-adjust lever with the ferocity of a fighter pilot ejecting from his cockpit after taking fire from a Russian MiG. Luckily, Sheryl did not to notice him. Desmond slowly crept his head up high enough to peer over the door through the window. As he did, he saw a man getting into Sheryl's passenger seat causing him to jolt back into a ducked position. When Desmond mustered enough stealthy nerve to peek again, he was just in time to see the front end of Sheryl's car rolling backward as she pulled out of the spot.

"Where the fuck?" Desmond mouthed.

Quickly he readjusted his seat and pulled out as well. His haste made the tires squeal slightly, but not enough to cause alarm. He saw Sheryl's car make a left turn at the light leading toward the outer edge of town. In a scramble. He sped up to catch the light before it turned red. Unfortunately for Desmond, this particular light seemingly had the shortest yellow in traffic light history and it turned red as he was approaching it. Decision time. He was racing too fast to stop. As were his mind and his heart. He threw his foot down on the gas and yanked the wheel hard to clear the on coming traffic. Horns blared declarations of war over his act of aggression. He made it through the light unscathed and just in time to see Sheryl's car about a block and a half up pull into a lot.

"Whoop! Whoop!" a cop appeared out of nowhere like the voice of conscience.

"Shit!" Desmond exclaimed.

He wanted to keep driving and, for a second, he played out the entire scenario in his head. It didn't end well. No, Desmond had to pull over and get this over with as quickly as possible so he can catch up to Sheryl and the guy she's fucking. He jolted the car into the shoulder and put it in park. He retrieved the rental paperwork from the glovebox and rolled down all of his windows. He took a few deep breaths and tried to adjust his posture and his facial expression to exude some semblance of calm on the outside even though he was an enraged ball of fire on the inside.

"How you doing, sir? Know why I pulled you over?" the officer asked.

Normally Desmond would play the *why no officer* game, but not today.

"Yea, I blew right through that red, didn't I? Sorry officer I got distracted and by the time I realized I felt like I either had to gun through it or slam on my brakes and get bashed by the car behind me,"

"License and registration?"

"This is a rental. Here is the rental doc and my license." Desmond offered.

"I'm not gonna find anything wrong when I run this, right? No points or anything?"

"Nope. I'm clean."

"Ok. Hold tight."

The seconds crawled by like hours as the cop moseyed to his patrol car. Again, Desmond fantasized about gunning the gas pedal. But that was just stupid. His mind and eyes darted around like crazy while he waited. Desmond focused his eyes on the area in which he saw Sheryl's car turn. It was tough to see clearly. A lot of cars going in and out or riding the shoulder to get somewhere faster.

(Shit! Was that Sheryl's car that just pulled out? Let's fucking go jerkoff!)

The cop came back after a few minutes.

"Gotta give you a moving violation because of where the intersection was, but I reduced it, so you don't get any points. You gotta make sure…" The cop continued talking, but Desmond stopped listening.

Under any normal circumstances, Desmond might have been more courteous, even grateful for the cop reducing the violation, but right now he didn't give a fuck about what the cop had to say.

(Just give me my ticket and fuck off already.)

The cop, seemingly reading Desmond's mind, obliged. He handed out the ticket and then, indeed fucked off back to his patrol car. Desmond waited an extra few seconds for the cop to pull away before he reengaged his mission. He didn't want the cop to end up behind him in traffic for the next block and then see where he pulled into in case the situation got out of hand.

Desmond pulled back into the slow lane and booked it down the street. Between his wife's utter betrayal, the noise in his head, the adrenaline, and the traffic stop, Desmond failed to take notice of where exactly he was headed. Realization, however, hit him like a hurricane wave crashing into a sand dune as he turned into the lot that Sheryl had turned into earlier. As he pulled up, he got dizzy. His car came to a halt. Before him was *the Top*. The hotel and restaurant where he and Sheryl had their first date.

27. Desmond's Past: Going in Circles

Desmond threw open the driver's side door and hurled himself from the seat so fast that his seatbelt didn't have time to fully retract. The shoulder strap caught his arm and pulled him backward as if to say, *don't go in there.* He shook free and rushed out into the parking lot. He moved across the aisle looking for Sheryl's car, but he couldn't find it. It had to be there. Desmond was certain that he saw her car pull into this lot. Or had he been so enraged that he saw it all wrong? He charged toward the entrance. Stumbling through the slowly spinning door, he landed in the front lobby of the hotel noisily gaining the attention of a few patrons and the hostess at the front desk, but he didn't give a fuck. His face and gait made that clear as he walked about the lobby, head on a tilt looking for his whoring wife and the scumbag with her.

Walking up to the check-in desk, Desmond pulled out his phone.

"Good afternoon, sir. Can I he-."

"Did this woman just come in here?" Desmond interrupted hastily.

"Sir?"

"This woman. Did. She. Just. Come in here. She was with a man."

I'm sorry sir. I didn't see-."

"Yea. Thanks anyway." Desmond spewed as he turned toward the elevators.

As he got to the elevators and pushed the up button, he was confronted by hotel security. The security guard was a slightly elderly man who was also slightly overweight. No gun. No taser. No cuffs. Not even a whistle. Just a regular old guy, probably retired, who wasn't good at sitting home watching daytime tv.

"Can I help you sir?"

"You have a gun?" Desmond fired back.

"Uh I uh." The guard stammered.

"Then not really." Desmond replied as the elevator door opened.

As they closed, he heard the security guard radio to the front desk to call the cops.

(Thanks a lot, gramps!)

Desmond paced inside the box as the elevator ascended. With each passing floor toward the top, Desmond grew more and more impatient and angry. His mind was wrecked. All he could see were flashes of his hands around the neck of whatever guy he found with his wife. Choking him on the ground while Sheryl looked on screaming and pleading, crying about the mistake she'd made.

(Too late, bitch!)

After what felt to Desmond like a stretch in purgatory, the elevator doors opened, and he stepped out into the lounge. Immediately he was hit with a nauseous feeling as the ultra-slow spin of the floor gripped his body. He moved counterclockwise around the outer perimeter of the lounge. The choice of direction was deliberate. It was the opposite direction of the spinning floor and it felt like the way a detective would move about the room. At tables scattered around the inner circle sat couples and groups of people all having the time of their lives. Laughter and smiles mocked Desmond's senses.

He made his way to the far end of the bar area, but Sheryl was nowhere in sight. He began to question whether he had seen Sheryl at all, or if he had just been following a rabbit. He needed a fucking drink. He sat at the bar and called the bartender over.

"Double whisky."

The bartender obliged and Desmond gulped it down with a deep breath. As he set the glass on the bar top his vision caught the elevators across the lounge. Sheryl was waiting by the door. With her was Desmond's best friend. Desmond stood. He wanted to yell. To run at them and tear them apart, but as he stood and stepped from the bar area, the movement of the room again caught him off guard and he wobbled a bit. He caught himself on the back of a high top table chair just in time to watch the elevator doors open. Two cops stepped off. Sheryl and his *friend* stepped in.

"Fuuuck." Desmond whispered under his breath.

He had to get out of there. He was pretty sure these two cops were there for him and not to tie one on after their shift. The cops stepped into the lounge and began to move clockwise around the perimeter. Fucking amateurs. Desmond did the same, keeping pace with their stride in an attempt not to draw attention.

(Christ! It's the same fucking cop that pulled me over.)

Though Desmond technically didn't do anything illegal, the last thing he needed was to get detained by this fucking guy again further screwing up his pursuit. As Desmond neared the elevators, he looked back to gauge his threat level. Luckily for him, the cops had sat down. It seems they were there to tie one on after all. Either that or they weren't particularly keen on conducting a manhunt. All the same to Desmond. He got in the elevator and pushed the button for the lobby.

"Drink it up, fellas." He said out loud to himself.

By the time Desmond got to the lobby it was just as it was when he'd first arrived. No sign of Sheryl or her car. It's like he was chasing a ghost. He sat on one of the oversized leather chairs at the edge of the lobby. He wasn't chasing ghosts. He knew what he saw.

(And I will catch them)

"But not this way." He said to himself.

Desmond took some time to walk himself down from the ledge, and then he came to a realization. An emotional, crime of passion style reaction wasn't the way he wanted to play this thing out. Where would be the fun in that. No, barging in on his wife cheating on him with his friend and tearing them apart like an out-of-control rage monster might feel good in the moment, but it was too abrupt. Too quick to the end result with not enough suffering for them in between. Plus, it would land him on death row and, as much as Desmond didn't feel like caring what happened to him afterward, the truth is, being locked up in a cage was about the only thing in this world that petrified him.

28. Desmond's Past: The plan

Desmond left the hotel parking lot and returned the rental. Then, after exchanging the rental back for his car, he drove home and walked in as if he hadn't just spent the day dressed in a masochists clothing. Sheryl was in the kitchen wearing the facade of a committed wife. She wore it well. When Desmond reached the doorway to the kitchen, Sheryl was quick with a hug and a kiss to welcome him home. Desmond did his best not to tense up, vomit, or scream.

They traded mild niceties and then Desmond went up to shower while Sheryl finished making dinner. Most of the night was a blur for Desmond. Sheryl yapped away about this and that while they ate and he nodded along on autopilot, looking for facial queues half-heartedly so he could mimic her expressions to not let on that he was completely in his head devising his plan.

Sheryl may have been finished with a story or just paused to take a mouthful of food when Desmond cut in.

"You know," he started. "I was thinking. My birthday is coming up and I thought it might be fun to charter a boat and invite some of the guys to go fishing for a few hours that morning." Knowing damn well he was only going to invite one *friend*.

He didn't wait for Sheryl's response before continuing.

"I actually already rented a boat. I figured you could take the morning for yourself. Whatta ya think?"

"Well, I suppose if you already rented the boat, you can't let it go to waste." Sheryl replied with a shrug.

Desmond expected some push back from Sheryl. He wanted it, but she didn't seem to mind or care which infuriated him. Desmond's insides were bubbling like the fires on the surface of the sun. On the outside he appeared as cool as the dark side of the moon. He knew he couldn't break his composure if he wanted everything to work out just so.

With her approval, he figured the rest of the plan would be easy. Set sail. Get somewhere out to sea. Confront this asshole, and then dispose of him.

(Ah yea. It's gonna be excellent.)

29. Shipwrecked: Bloody Hands

Desmond reached down into the water and scooped his bloody friend from the water. He landed with a groan and a thud into the hull. His gut was wrenched, and he was moaning in pain. Instinctually, Desmond reached into his bag to try to find something to stop the bleeding, or at least slow it down. For a moment while he was rummaging, Desmond paused. What if he'd just let him sit there and slowly bleed out. Then, his hands would be clean of the murder and the suffering would be immense.

"No." he reconsidered under his breath.

Although Desmond liked the idea of watching his *friend* suffer, he did not relish in the thought of him dying in a way other than what Desmond would dictate. He wanted the blood on his hands both figuratively and literally, and he would get his revenge. Refocusing, he grabbed the first aid kit that was inside the bag. Desmond's mate sat leaning back limply against the side of the boat.

"Wh-what was that, Des?"

"Sea beast." Desmond said through his teeth while he used them to pry open the plastic wrap which sealed the first aid kit. "Don't worry, chum. We'll patch you up right as rain."

Desmond opened the kit and retrieved all the gauze and the liquid antiseptic within. Luckily, this kit also had a small needle and some thread inside a separate little clear plastic baggy. Desmond held it up to the sun with a winning smile.

"Head back, mate. This is gonna sting a bit."

Desmond opened the antiseptic and began squeezing the contents directly onto his buddy's wounds in a gleeful, haphazard way like one of those viral videos of a drunk guy at a backyard barbeque showing off over a fire with a bottle full of lighter fluid.

"Aarhghah! Fuck! That hurts. You trying to kill me?"

Desmond knew that question was rhetorical and spontaneous because of the sting of the antiseptic. Still, it made him smile inside.

"Not yet mate." Desmond said honestly sounding as if in jest. "Gonna patch you up."

Desmond wiped away the emerging blood with one of the gauze pads, and with an over-the-top swipe, slapped the rest of the gauze down hard onto the wounds. They weren't quite as bad as they appeared, but still bad enough that if they went untreated, they could become lethal. Regardless, Desmond wasn't worried. He knew they'd neither be treated or become lethal. His *friend* wouldn't be around long enough for any of that.

He cut some cord to hold the gauze in place. Desmond stretched it around the torso and pulled it tight in a knot. His friend groaned, loudly. His painful cries decrescendoed across the open water like the wails of a sitar in a song of despair. Music to Desmond's ears. Desmond reached back into the bag and grabbed out the bottle with his pill inside. He held it up toward the sun and looked at it with one squinted eye as he rattled it.

"Here, mate. Take this." Desmond offered. He certainly wasn't going to fucking take it.

"Is it a pain killer?"

"It's a killer alright." Desmond said as he coaxed it into his friend's mouth.

Desmond then held up some water for his friend to drink. A few small whimpers followed, trailing off into murmurs. Desmond stood over his mate smiling. It was last thing he saw before passing out.

30. Shipwrecked: Rabbit's Foot

Desmond stood there staring down for a bit. His mind crashed with waves of rage. His eyes glazed like the haze of a post storm sky. He breathed in the salty air, deep and closed his eyes. In and out, his breath mimicked the rhythm of the ocean beneath. If observed by an outsider, one might think Desmond was at complete peace. A yogi in a meditative state. They'd be right to some degree. Outwardly, he was completely tranquil. His peace, however, was not achieved with a clear mind. His outward appearance of serenity was achieved from the repeated images of standing over the completely obliterated body of the man who wrecked his life.

Desmond opened his eyes and got to work. He grabbed the rest of the cord and used it to tie up his soon to be victim. Then, he waited. Much of the day passed as the men continued to drift across the open water. Though his friend was still unconscious, a few groans of pain would emanate from where he was tied at the far end of the boat. Sitting back against the boats edge, Desmond whistled a tune. His thumb and forefinger were at his side, between them he rolled the rabbit's foot he kept on a small rope attached to his beltloop.

This motion caused him to drift into some of his earliest memories. He was just about to descend into one when his somewhat gutted friend came to with a groan. Desmond's head cocked up and to the side. Eyes scrunched from the sun and his distain.

"Des?" His mate asked. " I-I'm hurtin'. I, I don't feel too good. That pill. It didn't help. I feel…fuzzy."

After a long pause Desmond responded. "Ok chum. You'll be right as rain soon enough."

Looking down toward his belly, he could see the hastily stitched wounds. The edges of them were discolored. An array of reds and purples. A bit of filmy, yellowish discharge had run out of the base and dried in a line like excess paint on a shoddily painted wall.

"I dunno, Des. If we don't get rescued, I don't think I'm gonna make it." He said to Desmond hoping for reassurance.

"Not in this world, mate." Desmond said plainly.

"W-What?"

"Do you know what this is?" Desmond held up his rabbit's foot.

Confusion set in on his boatmates face and before he could answer, Desmond flashed into his childhood memories without regard.

■ ■

Desmond was about four or five when he got the stuffed rabbit from his mother. She gave him the present right before putting him to bed for the night and told him it would protect him from anything that would try to harm him.

"Give him a name, sweetie, and he'll protect you, always."

He didn't quite understand but, at four or five, when your mother tells you something, you believe it. She tucked Desmond in an turned off the light. Desmond sat up in bed and stared at the rabbit. The darkness of the room turned it into somewhat of a silhouette. Its features were mostly obscured except its eyes. The rabbit had these glossy brown button eyes. What little light shined into the room from behind the window curtain reflected off them with a milky glow, hypnotic like an angler fish.

Desmond wanted to give the rabbit a scary name. In his boyish logic, a rabbit with a scary name would be much better at protecting him. He decided to call the rabbit, Monster. After all, what was scarier than a monster? He'd heard his mother call his father that often, and she always seemed pretty scared.

His father had a drinking problem. He'd come home from the bar in town late and loud. And on those frequent nights, he'd come home pissed off at the world. On those frequent nights, he'd take his anger out on Desmond and his mother.

In attempts to spare Desmond from his father's onslaughts, she'd lock Desmond in a small coat closet at the end of the hall. It was dark and smelly. Full of mostly unused junk from a time that passed. The back wall was on an angle. It came down into a V shape. Desmond would hide behind the coats and whatnot as far back as he could squeeze.

He was small and weak. From the closet he could hear his mother pleading and screaming. Echoes of knuckles across her cheek would splinter through the door. Desmond loathed himself for never doing something to protect her. He just couldn't bring himself to go out there. Instead, he'd ball up in the back where it was the darkest.

That's when Monster would talk to him.

From the utter darkness, Monster would whisper in his ear. Almost inaudibly at first. Mumblings from an inanimate object. The fright filled delusions of a small child. His whispers would persist growing louder and louder until they turned to roars, howling something over and over again that Desmond couldn't quite make out, but it drowned out the screams from the other side of the door until consuming his senses and it was more than he could bare. Then, in a flash, Desmond would wake up to find himself back in his bed, as if awakening from a terrible nightmare. Each time, he'd grab Monster and scramble to find his mother. Usually, he'd find her in the kitchen making coffee. Face plastered in makeup. She and the birds chirping as if nothing had ever happened.

That's how it went on Bea St. Night after night, Desmond's father would come home drunk and angry. Night after night, Desmond's mother would take a beating. Night after night, Desmond would cower in the back of the closet as the rumblings from his stuffed rabbit muffled their screams. Night after night, until the last night.

On the last night, Desmond woke up in the middle of the night, but not in his bed. He was in the grass. It was dewy and pointy, itching his skin. A warm glow emanated from behind him. Slowly, he sat up clutching Monster. It took him a few minutes to fully wake up and see it. He was in his front yard. A beautiful amber glow lit up the sky around him. His house was a blazing hellfire. Billows of smoke escaped from every window, every crevice. The wood crackled and moaned as the flames consumed it from the inside. Sirens in the distance grew louder and louder. All of it assaulting his senses.

Desmond stood and ran toward the house screaming for his mom. Maybe the first brave thing he ever did. He didn't have a plan, just a compulsion. When he made it about ten yards or so from the porch, the house exploded tossing him and his stuffed rabbit into the air like leaves in the wind. They hurdled across the yard to the ground, hitting it with a thud. Then, everything went black again.

Desmond awoke three days later from a coma screaming for his mother while doctors and nurses scrambled about. According to the official report, neither Desmond's mother nor his father made it out of the fire alive. The explosion rendered the house and everything inside it almost completely indistinguishable, though some burnt ashy flesh and bone fragments were recovered. They never did figure out how Desmond ended up in the grass or just how the fire started, but Desmond still believes it was Monster on both accounts.

. .

Many minutes passed as Desmond sat there with a thousand-yard stare. Far off in the distance, lightning flashed across the sky like cameras from a relentless paparazzi. Thunder began to rumble.

Desmond took in a large breath. His boatmate let out a loud exhale. Both men were shaking.

"Desmond. What the fuck?"

The question brought Desmond back from the distance. He looked at his boatmate and continued as if he'd never drifted off.

"It's a rabbit's foot." He exclaimed. "But this here isn't from just any old rabbit. No sir. This one is special."

Rumblings from the sky slowly grew closer, looming like a cliché overhead. The water was beginning to get turbulent, and the boat was rocking deeply in a wobbly motion.

"Anyway." Desmond said dismissively as if on a pivot. "Hell of a predicament you find yourself in, eh mate?"

"You know why you're here."

The statement had Desmond's friend at a loss.

"You're here, chum, because you fucked my wife."

The shock on his friend's face was a convincing performance.

"I what?" He questioned in denial. "What are you talking about?"

The storm seemed imminent. Desmond was astutely aware that the time for him to exact his revenge was running short. He wasn't going to let anything, neither storm nor sea creature, stop him from finishing what he'd started. He reached for his knife and brandished it with a grin. The confusion on his friend's face turned to fear.

"Desmond. I didn't!" Is all he could utter in his weakened state.

"Yea…you fucked her alright and now you're fucked."

Desmond didn't waste another minute on useless conversation. He knew it was all leading to the same place. Him driving his serrated combat-style knife deep into the belly of the pig in front of him.

"I'll do it myself this time." Desmond said aloud to no one.

His friend began to holler and swing his arms with what little strength he could muster. Then Desmond stood up, leaned in, and thrusted his knife into his mate's midsection. Over and over and over again.

31. The Island: Who Are You?

Sam couldn't believe his own eyes. How the fuck did the boat get way out here in the jungle? He knew the answer to that question, though. Looking at Desmond, it was impossible for Sam to hide his rage.

Desmond was about to speak when Sam cocked back and swung at him with everything he had. The blow blasted across Desmond's eye socket causing his head to jar back. Sam's fist recoiled uncontrollably but he kept swinging as both men fell to the ground.

They were rolling around like animals, exchanging punches as a crowd of howling monkeys grew around them in the trees, shaking the branches and screaming blood curdling screams. Both men were also screaming and grunting, belligerently. Sam in accusation. Desmond in protest.

Desmond's knife was in play as well. Both he and Sam were grappling for it from Desmond's belt loop. After a long tussle, Sam gained the upper hand and hit Desmond squarely in his nose. The back of Desmond's head bounced hard off the ground. Sam found his footing and yanked the knife from Desmond's waist and pointed it down at Desmond. The blood crusted blade glistened in the light.

"Stay down!" Sam screamed, kicking Desmond in his side.

"You crazy motherfucker." Sam screamed. "You dragged the boat out here?"

"The b-boat?" Desmond questioned between groans.

"You son-of-a-bitch! Who the fuck are you? What's in the boat, Desmond?"

"Sam…Listen. Don't go to-"

Sam interrupted Desmond with a kick across his face. Blood splashed across the ground. The howls from the trees permeated the jungle like a siren, warning of an impending apocalypse. Desmond was laying limply in the dirt reaching his arm out in a failed attempt to grab onto Sam's leg as he went passed. Sam began to hobble down the side of the ridge along a narrow path on the far side of the hill where he saw the boat. His knee was throbbing, and blood was seeping from his face. The dirt on the path was loose and scattered with small stones and underdeveloped coconut spathes making it slippery and uneven.

With every step, Sam felt as if he were teetering on the edge of the Earth. He made it about a quarter of the way down the slope when Desmond tackled him from behind. Sam's back folded nearly in half from the impact and the knife flung from his hand disappearing into the thick vines below. Both men tumbled down the side of the ridge toward the jungle floor. Entangled in a death lock, they exchanged punches, pulls, and bites as they descended. Their momentum was unrelenting, propelling them chaotically into tree trunks and rocks along the way.

The side of Sam's head slammed into a rock about halfway down causing him to momentarily blackout. The hit caused a flash of a memory from one of the stories that Desmond told on the beach. It was like a dream. Sam was on a roof, tumbling off it. For a moment, it felt like he was actually there. Then, just as suddenly as it came, the vision was gone, and Sam was continuing his fall down the side of the hill. They ricocheted like pinballs off everything in their path until they reached the bottom.

Sam's head was spinning. Struggling to get to his feet, he saw Desmond doing the same. It took several minutes for either of them to get to up. Sam was heaving breaths and spitting blood. His insides felt crushed and rearranged.

"Sam. Listen, mate." Desmond began. "Just forget this and go back to the beach. We'll sort it out there."

Sam heard what Desmond said, but it wasn't registering. Nothing was going to get in his way of getting to that boat. Neither berms nor sharp sticks. Monsters nor blackouts. He had no desire to talk anymore. Sam lunged at Desmond and the men began to tussle again. Sam wrestled his way on top and began wailing on Desmond.

An eruption went off in Sam's head. A bright light blurred his vision. He continued to swing erratically. As he did, he kept flashing back and forth from his present to visions he'd had before. He, suddenly, was back at some outdoor café with a woman who he couldn't quite see but knew was familiar.

FLASH!

He was pounding Desmond's head into the ground.

FLASH!

The jungle floor turned to cobblestone and there was a glow from streetlights above. The smell of pastries was in the air.

FLASH!

Desmond's face was almost unrecognizable from the blood and swelling. Sam continued to pummel.

FLASH!

The woman was giggling from a seat across the table from Sam. He could smell her. She was almost in focus. She put her hand on his, and then he saw her.

"SHERYL!" Sam screamed out loud without fully understanding why.

FLASH!

Sam was strangling Desmond, shaking him violently trying to squeeze out whatever life he had left. Bursting flashes kept pulling

Sam in and out of two realities. He needed it to end. His eyes were closed tightly trying to block out everything that was in front of him and everything within his head. Reaching into his pocket, he dug out the toothbrush-knife he kept within it and began thrusting it rapidly into Desmond's midsection. Desperate howls penetrated the skies. He stabbed and stabbed until he could no longer lift his arms.

Heaving from exhaustion, he opened his eyes slowly. Almost frightened of the bloodbath he created. His eyes were closed so tightly that they needed to readjust to the light. When he finally gained vision back, he saw it.

Nothing. There was nothing there. No blood other than his own. Nobody was there on the jungle floor except for him and a log in which his makeshift knife was stuck.

He didn't understand what was happening to him. The trees began to spin. The disorientation he felt from it caused him to fall back onto his ass and he put his hands over his eyes, shaking his head uncontrollably in disbelief. As he sat there, a stream of memories flooded his mind like an intravenous drug. The fire. The college. Daffodils. Sheryl and her cheating. The boat and the murder. He screamed out to the sky.

(This isn't possible! It's insane!)

He wasn't completely sure what was real and what was a fabrication of his mind. Suddenly, he knew who he was and what had transpired. He wasn't Sam at all. This revelation was maddening.

A rustling in the brush nearby caught his attention. Desmond pulled his hands from in front of his eyes to see what was approaching. A small rabbit emerged from the brush and hopped onto the log in front of him. It stared Desmond in the eyes, seeing all the way into him. Desmond stared back at the rabbit and, for the first time, understood everything.

Without a sound, the rabbit leapt down from the log. It looked back at Desmond, urging him to come with it.

"Ok, Monster." Desmond said in a sighed breath.

He got up and followed the rabbit. It led him to the boat. Desmond glowered at it, knowing what he'd uncover inside. He took the few remaining steps toward it until he was standing right over the gunwale. The putrid stench was palpable. Inside the boat lay the remains of his former best friend. The man who wrecked his marriage. His boatmate. It was Sam. Bones mostly picked clean by the monsters within the jungle.

Desmond smiled. "Hey old chum. You're looking worse for the wear, eh?"

He reached down into the boat and grabbed his bag. Opening it to take inventory, he found what it was he needed. The flare gun and flare. He loaded the flare into the gun and stuck it into his waist. He emptied the rest of the contents on the jungle floor. They fell with a thud. One of the items, the novel Sheryl snuck in there, opened to where the pages had been ripped out when it hit the ground. He looked down at it, and then knelt to pick it up. As he did, he noticed a note written on the inside of the back cover. A huffed snicker shot from his mouth, and he stood back up leaving the book where it landed and left the note unread. He kicked it closed.

(Can't finish something you never started.)

With the bag empty in one hand, he grabbed Sam's remains piece by piece and threw him haphazardly inside. They rattled and clanged like a wooden windchime. Saving Sam's skull for last, he held it up into a ray of light streaming between the trees. He tilted it side to side in his hand in examination, listening for the echoes of Sam's voice. Then he chucked it inside with the rest of the skeleton. Zipping the bag, he looked down at the rabbit who was perched at the edge of the clearing.

"Alright then." He said to it. "Time to go."

Then, he cracked his neck and slung the bag over his shoulder. Whistling an off-tune melody, he began to make his way back to the beach. The rabbit hopped off into the jungle and then disappeared.

32. The Island: Awaiting Rescue

Desmond sat on the beach waiting for the arrival of the rescue boat. When he made his way back from the jungle, he waited at the water's edge until he saw, in the distance, an aircraft. He fired the flare into the sky and watched it as it exploded in celebration, then drifted in smoke back toward the Earth. The aircraft acknowledged seeing the flare by circling back toward the island and doing a flyby.

The night was approaching, and Desmond spent his last hours on the beach indulging in the memories of the events that lead him there. He knew what he needed to do. Recalling his initial plan, he started to think about how he was going to play out the next part of his life. Would he tell the tale of his friend, Sam the hero, and how if it weren't for Sam, he wouldn't have made it as long as he had?

No. The real Sam didn't deserve any reverence. A tragic accident at sea. Seemed simple enough. Sam died from exposure on the lifeboat. It was completely plausible and there was no reason to establish some elaborate story.

(Why didn't you just leave him in the boat? Why didn't you bury him?)

Desmond figured that these questions along with a million others were sure to come up at some point. He could simply say burying Sam was too much to bear. Regardless, he decided he'd just wing it and go with the moment when these situations arose. There really wasn't any way he could fuck it up in his estimation as long as whatever he said to the authorities wasn't the truth.

Perhaps no one would ever really know what Sam did or what fate ended his life. Though, Sheryl might suspect. Desmond hadn't fleshed that part out. He was torn. Initially, he killed his friend for revenge. To satisfy what he felt was a justifiable punishment for coveting his wife. The aftermath of which, never came into full view in his imaginings. What did he want? What did he expect would unfold? A happily ever after? Could he bury everything that transpired on the boat and the island right there in the jungle and continue as if it never occurred? That seemed unlikely if not impossible. Desmond certainly wanted Sheryl to know that he knew what she and Sam did. He concluded that there was no coming back from that. It's funny where lines are drawn in the mind of a madman. That the idea of Sheryl knowing Desmond found out she cheated. That was the point from which Desmond believed a couple couldn't recover. Never mind the cheating itself, or the murder. It would be the mutual knowledge between them of Sheryl's infidelity that would be the final unravelling of their marriage.

Regardless, this type of knowledge doesn't stay buried forever. Things like cuckoldry and killings tend to be revealed. It didn't matter that, in his own mind, he still loved Sheryl or that there was actually a part of him that was remorseful for the way things had to turn out. Eventually, Desmond knew, he'd say something or do something that would tip his hat and she'd realize the truth of what she'd probably suspect anyway. Ultimately dooming any chance of a happy ending.

After hours wandering inside his head, he saw a light moving toward the island from the open water. He got up from the sand and began pacing side to side waving his arms to let the captain know that he was headed in the right direction.

From the vessel approached a small helicopter. Spotlights shone from it like beams from a UFO in the midst of an obduction as it hovered toward the island. Desmond, though still completely torn up from the jungle, hustled best he could over to it as it settled down onto the sand. Three men disembarked to initiate the rescue. It was loud and time moved in blurred flashes. Men running up to Desmond. Handshakes. Wrapped in an oversized blanket. Vitals. Loud talking into a headset. Helped onto the helicopter. Loud talking into a headset. Helped down into the rescue boat. A piping hot coffee. Cheering over a headset. Overwhelming exhaustion. Blacking out. Waking up in the middle of the night as the boat approached the dock on the mainland.

The boat was fifty yards or so from the dock when Desmond made his way to the bow. On the dock, people were gathered. Floodlights from news crews had the entire area lit up like day.

Adrenaline shot through Desmond's veins. Somewhere on that dock, Sheryl was waiting. The scene was much like he'd imagined it. When the boat docked, it was flooded with people. Emergency workers, police, and reporters. Commotion filled the air, thick and raucous. Desmond cut through the crowd and chopped through the noise until he saw her. Sheryl was standing in close proximity to some police officers, yet at the same time alone. Arms folded, wearing a jacket that was not quite shielding her from the coolness of the breeze. Hair undone, no makeup. She looked exactly the way you'd picture a wife who is about to be reunited with her husband after she'd feared the worst. The man she loved so dearly.

(a grand façade)

Sheryl was standing at the back end of the crowd unable to push forward. Desmond continued toward her and, as he did, he was bombarded with a swell of emotions all in combat with one another. As much rage as he had burning inside of him, he also felt tremendous relief. When he emerged from the crowd, Sheryl ran up to him and wrapped her arms around him tightly. By virtue of his height, the embrace lifted Sheryl from her feet. Videos streamed into live broadcasts like the finale of a reality tv show. Cameras from the newspapers snapped relentlessly, making hundreds of memories of that single moment. Proclamations of love reunited were made over breaking news headlines.

"Desmond. I. I-" Sheryl started.

"I know." Desmond said before she could finish.

(I know more than you think)

33. A New Start

Desmond and Sheryl were transported to the hospital where he was treated for his minor injuries, given fluids, and a few doses of anti-parasitics to be on the safe side. After being given an all clear from the doctors, Desmond had to make official statements down at the police station. For now, the police seemed satisfied with the stories that Desmond fed them regarding the fishing expedition he and Sam embarked on. Their treacherous bout with the open sea, and the ordeal Desmond faced *alone* on the island. Ironically, his plan to disable the GPS and head out in the opposite direction of his itinerary worked so well that it rendered search party efforts ineffective.

Sheryl decided not to inundate Desmond with questions of her own just yet. She couldn't imagine the mental trauma he was dealing with, and she didn't want to add to it. She was obviously unaware of the irony of it all. Instead, she focused on simply staying by Desmond's side, and offering loving, physical contact in attempts to provide some form of comfort.

With the check up in the hospital and the official statement documented at the police station, it was time to head home. A short flight, during which both Desmond and Sheryl slept. Desmond dreamt.

■ ■

In his dream he and Sheryl were home, sitting on their porch. It was midday and the few clouds in the sky were puffy white. A sprinkler was swaying back and forth across the greenest grass he'd ever laid eyes on. The sweet scent of flowers wafted into the air with the breeze. They were much older, though Sheryl was still radiant. She glowed with a warmth which Desmond hadn't felt in longer than he could remember. He basked in it eyes closed.

■ ■

Desmond awoke as the plane was landing. His dream left him in a state of contented relief. Perhaps, he and Sheryl could find their way back to their happy ending after all. He looked over at Sheryl. His contentedness dissipated. Dreams tainted by realities.

A police escort brought them to their house. As they approached, Desmond took everything in. The lawn was overgrown in patches. Weeds grew through flowers in the beds along the base of their porch. As they walked toward their front door, Sheryl held him tightly. It reminded him of how she held him when they were just dating. Back when her gestures were true. Unsullied by the stench of her betrayals. Outwardly, Desmond appeared to be contented by her touch. Inside, though, his stomach was churning with acidic volatility.

Desmond paused at the threshold. An odor offensive to his senses filled the air. Looking down at the flower beds he saw them. Daffodils. A whole row of them with their bulbs facing the ground. They were neglected and dying.

"Des?" Sheryl asked from the door which she'd just opened.

"You ok?"

"Right as rain." Desmond replied lowly.

Together they went inside.

"Darlin'. Sheryl began. "Why don't you take a shower." And I'll put fresh sheets down on the bed."

Desmond nodded, and then turned to go upstairs to the bedroom. Sheryl grabbed his arm to halt him and kissed him on the cheek.

"Welcome home." She smiled

It felt like a lifetime ago the last time Desmond was in their house. Sheryl went off to the laundry room to get the bed sheets. Desmond walked slowly from the foyer to the stairs. Along the way, he stopped at the entryway table. On it was a key tray, and a small, framed photo. He picked up the frame to examine it. It was a picture of he and Sheryl. They looked young. He couldn't quite remember where the photo was taken, but it must have been somewhere special to them. The silence in the house was in direct contrast to the clatter in his head. He was suddenly very aware of this chaotic anomaly. With a shrug, he put the frame back and headed toward the shower.

From the shower, he could here Sheryl in the bedroom tidying up and fixing the bed. She came into the bathroom as well to let Desmond know she put a fresh towel on the rack for him. The water was running very hot. Desmond stood beneath it allowing everything to wash over and away from him. Steam filled the bathroom in a thick plume. After a while, he turned off the shower. The mirror was coated in condensation. Before him on the counter was his straight razor. Desmond always liked the way the single blade felt against his skin. His beard, of course, was overgrown so before he could shave, he trimmed it down with his buzzer. He lathered his face and wiped a streak across the mirror with a hand towel revealing just enough of the mirror to reflect his face in a blur. In the reflection, he watched as seemingly all the events of his life played out in front of him. Desmond was deep into these scenes when Sheryl began talking to him from the other room. As it happens when people are reunited after a long time, particularly after a tragedy, Sheryl had a lot to say.

"Desmond, darlin'." She started. "I thought I'd lost you forever and it wrecked me. I didn't know what I'd do without you. I prayed and prayed they would find you after you disappeared…"

Sheryl continued without a breath. Desmond faded in and out catching a few words here and there, but mostly stared blankly into the mirror.

I love you blah blah blah...Clean slate blah blah blah...so many things I want to tell you blah blah blah.

While she went on, Desmond put the razor to his face to shave. He made long, slow, deliberate passes with the blade. His face, in spots, began to bleed slightly as he mindlessly pressed too hard. Then he saw it in the mirror. Staring at him almost mockingly as if to say, *you know what needs to be done.*

(Monster?)

Desmond dropped the razor. It clanged around in the sink, splashing watered down blood onto the counter. He turned. Sitting there on a shelf across from the vanity, it sat. It wasn't Monster. It was, however, a new version of the stuffed animal that Desmond had for most of his life. In its lap was a card.

"I left you a surprise on the shelf in there..." She continued

With his hands still wet from the water and blood, he grabbed the card. Inside it read:

'I'm grateful you found your way back to me.'

-M.A.D.

The ambient noise surrounding him grew louder. The water still running from the faucet, the ceiling fan, and Sheryl. All blending into a vexing ensemble of sounds. Then, all at once, they were silenced. Replaced only by the steady mummering within his own mind. He stared down at this new Monster. He stood there naked, bleeding, motionless. Listening intently as the murmurs grew into rumblings. Chants of rage were consuming his rationality. Reverberating like a virus through his veins. When, suddenly, Sheryl's voice broke back through.

"Desmond?" Sheryl called. "Did you hear me? I said I know I've been talking so much. I'm sorry. When you are ready, I want to know whatever you can tell me about what happened, Darlin'. Like what it was like." Sheryl knew her word choice was clunky.

"What it was like?" Desmond said steadily from the bathroom.

"Come to bed and whenever you are ready." She said sincerely.

Desmond put down the rabbit and grabbed the razor. Still undressed he walked out of the bathroom and into the bedroom where Sheryl was sitting on the bed. He stood in the doorway, an almost gory spectacle.

"Desmond?" Sheryl nearly shrieked in confused panic.

"What it was like?" He repeated.

"It was fun." He said with an odd grin. Then, he shot her a wink.

Epilogue

Later, on the night Desmond saw the email draft.

Sheryl got home before Desmond. She went straight up to the office to send out an email she had started to type earlier but didn't get to finish because she didn't want to raise suspicion.

She'd met with Sam twice before and they were having an incredible time. The first time they met was about a week earlier during their respective lunch breaks. It was more of a quick get together as they didn't have much time. The second time they met was the day prior to her drafting the email. Both she and Sam made sure they had plenty of time for that rendezvous.

Sheryl knew she had a lot to do, and she had to make sure Desmond wouldn't find out. If he did, it would ruin everything, and she exerted too much time and energy into keeping this a secret to allow it to be wrecked by him. To that end, Sheryl thought that the best way to correspond without getting caught was via email as opposed to texts. Texts can come in at inopportune times and unravel secrets.

When she got to the office, she hadn't noticed anything out of place, though if she were being discerning, she might have seen that the laptop was shifted off center from the dust line on the desk. Then, she would have made the connection that Desmond was snooping around and, perhaps, that would have let her in on the fact that Desmond was already on to her.

Opening the screen of the laptop, Sheryl saw that her browser was left open. A light panic set in momentarily. Had she been so careless as to leave her browser open? She must have, she convinced herself, noting that she needs to be less careless. After opening her email, she went into her drafts. There she found the message she'd started.

>*Yesterday was fun. ;)*

Knowing she didn't have much time; she hastily wrote out the email adding a greeting.

Hey Sam,

Yesterday was fun. ;)

Thank you for coming with me to check out the band for Desmond's surprise party. He is going to be so blown away that I was able to pull this all off without him finding out.

I just need your help with one more thing. Could we meet up maybe next week or so at the Top hotel lounge? As you know, that is where Desmond and I had our first date and I want to book it for our event.

Thanks again,

Sheryl.

Sheryl read her email to make sure there were no typos before sending it. It looked good, but she decided to remove the winky face at the top. No need for it, she thought. Besides, seemingly innocuous gestures can sometimes be taken the wrong way and wreck things.